The Pepsi-Cola Addict.

The Pepsi-Cola Addict by June-Alison Gibbons
© 2023 Strange Attractor Press; second printing

Text © 1981, 1982, 2022, and 2023 June-Alison Gibbons
Afterword © 2023 Chris Mikul

This edition originally published by Ania Goszczyńska and
David Tibet, with the full collaboration of June-Alison Gibbons,
at Cashen's Gap, 2022, in a hardback printing of 300 copies,
including a bookplate numbered and signed by the author.

Cover Design by Ania Goszczyńska
Text layout by Maïa Gaffney-Hyde
Typeset in Caslon & Bunyan Pro

Inside cover photograph by Maria Jefferis
Model: Freddie White

ISBN: 9781913689711

Strange Attractor Press
BM SAP
London, WC1N 3XX
UK

Distributed by The MIT Press, Cambridge, Massachusetts.
And London, England.
Printed and bound in the USA by Sheridan Saline, Inc.

The Pepsi- Cola Addict.

June-Alison gibbons.

PEPSI- COLA
ADDS LIFE

PEPSI- COLA
ADDS A little
Life.

[signature]
27/10/21

Intro—

My Idea to write this
book came when I
kept school Age 16yrs,
old. I wanted to
write about a boy
with a strange
peculiarity, hence an
addiction to a well
known sweet bevarage'
along with his nervous
antics which attract
strange people came
a book about a very
strange boy.
I hope you enjoy
reading this story as
much as I enjoyed
writing it. Enjoy!!!!
Best wishes, June-Alison Gibbons

For Jennifer.

He walked into the turbulent super market. There were people everywhere. His eyes swept over the shelves and stabilised on a large stack of Pepsi-colas. He could almost experience the cool fizzy liquid descending his parched throat. Feeling a heavy hand on his shoulder he turned around to meet the intellectual face of Mr. Rodell, one of the store clerks.

"Same as usual, huh?"

"I'll have them in bulk please."

"You into having some kind of party?"

He accompanied Mr. Rodell to the drinks quarter.

"I'll give you a box, okay?"

"Sure." Excavating into his Wrangler jacket he produced a five dollar note.

"Thanks son; have a nice day."

Carrying the hefty box along the sandy sidewalk, he desired right now to sit down, open a can of pepsi, and take a long swig. When he reached home he directly went to the refrigerator and arranged the thirty two cans of pepsi lengthwise on the exposed shelf. Then, taking three cans with him he headed for his room. He reclined on his bed.

Preston Wildey-King was a thin shouldered, narrow-waisted boy, with the muscular leanness and effortless grace of an athlete. His hair was brown, his eyes brown too; they slanted downwards to give his gaunt face a peculiar oriental expression.

The tenement in which he lived with his mother and sister was alternatively too hot or too cold. This room remained suffocatingly hot with the contained heat of the day. Preston was thinking he was cold. His head felt neurotic and dizzy. It resembled ice. He thought he wouldn't mind if he lived in Arizona, or even Hawaii; they lived on cool beverages and didn't care what you did. Sitting in his own pad and sipping 300 cans of pepsi cola every day. The thought made him thirsty. He was thirsty.

He swallowed some more pepsi, shifted his position, and his eyes commenced to wander around.

There was subtle colour in his bedroom; sable bricks beside yellow brimstone drawers, beside wood painted livid red. There was colour in the faces too, overlapping, blending and clashing so that the entire room displayed a world of zany pop singers. Style impassioned his thoughts in the form of pink graffiti that illuminated the name "PEGGY" ten times on the freshly painted white door.

Since the baseball match Preston had never felt so resolute. The thoughts of the fresh and wholesome cheerleader threatened to dominate his thoughts on pepsi cola. So he repressed his love and drank his inevitable life saver. When Peggy fell for a super jock in grade 8 he was emotionally turned inside out.

Preston, nonchalant about his aspect of life, was probably and accountably turning into a pepsi-cola addict. At fourteen years old wherever he turned, he somehow failed to develop any sense of adventure and remained statically serene with the drink he called the "high life". To him pepsi cola was like shallow water to a fish.

He closed his eyes. A radio blared from within the density of the bedroom walls, the disc jockey's rapid voice riding in and out over the rock and roll beat as he extolled the merits of the long top forty. The faint buzz of a spray. The knocking around next door revealed to Preston that his sister Erica was about to go out with one of her wise-cracking macho-type boy friends. How many she dated in a week Preston was unaware, but suspicious. She rarely seemed to be content with staying indoors, either attending some freak dancing club or dwelling in her high school buddy's pad for a night or two.

Most of the time she was compatible with Preston. Other times she joshed him and yelled. Preston felt easy when he was free of her loud, excessive reproaches. He seemed relieved to have her out, and out of his way.

He thought that she must be standing flauntingly beside her mirror, spraying sandalwood or jasmine over her sun-tanned wrists, just like Peggy occasionally did. This kind of life had dominated Erica since she was thirteen, and it was only a year before that that she was still associated with baby bean dolls. Preston shrugged his shoulders. This was one thing he disliked about sisters, they always grew up too rapidly.

An abrupt clamour at the front door reached his ears, and Preston impetuously sat up. A moment later the slightly made-up face of Erica was peering down at him.

"Wind up Prezz, Ryan's out back." She whispered urgently.

Preston's face changed. "Tell him I'm sleeping, okay?"

She extended her arm and clasped Preston's shoulders. "You're wide awake. Now get up."

"I'm asleep, tell him I'm asleep."

Erica flounced out the room, her reminiscent perfume lingering superfluously.

He lay there for a while listening to Ryan's distant footsteps, then turned over to his flatulent stomach, where he passively slept.

When he awoke the air was tranquil and the sun was shining. Smiling, he thought of Ryan. Ryan, his best buddy, his brother. He wistfully wanted to be beside him, so he got up and prepared for school.

Drinking a pepsi as he walked he visualised Ryan's lean form waiting by the intersection. They looked at each other seriously for a while, then Ryan's dolorous face broke into a smile. They walked in silence to the entrance of 'MALIBU STATE SCHOOL'.

"You didn't come to the beach party yesterday. Why not?"

Preston shrugged his shoulders and looked at a group of girls. "I wasn't up to it. Besides, I was tired."

"We hit off okay. They were into dust. It's kinda fun you know." When they reached the lockers Preston put in his cans of pepsi. They were revising Mrs. Rosenberg's math assignment when Ryan's face touched Preston's. "I saw your friend Peggy."

"Where was she?" Preston kept his eyes down.

"She was on the beach with Curt Miller. I went by they were having a quiet time."

He looked up. Ryan wasn't looking at him. "What were they doing?"

"I didn't see much. I was drunk."

'Tell me what they were doing."

"I don't know," Ryan whispered. "I just seen 'em together."

"How come you knew it was them?"

"I saw 'em."

"I thought you said you were drunk. You didn't see them."

"Oh year, I saw 'em."

"Who was it with her?" Preston asked.

"Curt Miller."

"Were they....." Preston stared at his pen. Closed his eyes. "Were they.... ?"

"Were they what?"

"Were they looking happy?"

"I guess so."

Mrs. Rosenberg's audible voice trembled the quiet room. "You have a problem, Preston? If you do, it'd be wiser if you stand right up and explain it to the rest of the fellow students. We'd all like to hear which sum you're stuck on."

On arriving home Preston's white tee shirt was literally clinging to his back. Erica was straddling below with a few of her groupie friends. Mrs. Wildey-King was just finishing the Pot Roast.

"Had a nice day Preston?"

"The usual," he pulled the ring and sipped the pepsi cola.

"You hungry?"

Preston was thinking of Peggy.

"Hey." Mrs. Wildey-King turned around. "You really do impress me Preston. Are you hungry?"

"What?.... Yeah I'm hungry." Preston felt confused. He ambled to his room peeling his tee shirt from his back.

Erica was at the table and serving out when he appeared later.

"Well now, where do you think you're going?"

"I'm taking a walk to the beach."

"And you made momma go through a hell of a lot of trouble to make your dinner and....."

Mrs. Wildey-King motioned her hand in the air to silence Erica. She gazed at her son openly. "Go on then." She sat down then with the dish cloth slung over her shoulder and watched as Preston, bare backed, pepsi in his hand, walked out.

Some Beatniks passed by on a Greyhound waving at him. Preston lingered by a dime store and in the reflected window he saw a familiar figure; a slap on the back told him it was Ryan.

"Where you headed?"

Preston rubbed the stinging sensation and swished his tee shirt around Ryan's head. "To the beach." They dodged the oncoming crowds. Ryan wasted a quarter on a dislodged weed machine. There was sand in his hair as Preston sauntered over to the lapping waves. When he lay down the sand burned him. Ryan gazed at his dismal expression.

"Hey what fazes you?"

Preston lay statically and closed his eyes.

"Hey are you still in love with Peggy, is that it?"

He opened his eyes. Ryan had changed.

"I notice you get pretty mad whenever I mention her, right?"

"Wrong." The slap of the waves made the place seem forlorn.

"What is it you like about her?"

"I just like her, no questions asked. Okay?"

Ryan extended his arm to rest on Preston's stomach. "You're through with her, what good is it you thinking of her like you were sick?"

"I'm all to feeling mad at her for going out with Curt Miller, but I just can't seem to get her out of my mind."

"You still feel something for her?" There was a strange look in Ryan's large black eyes. "You love her, don't you?"

Preston moved his arm gently and sat up. "Gee Ryan, you're my best friend, but what's it to you if I still love her?" he laughed drily. "I always make nice with girls anyway."

"I just don't wanna see you get hurt, that's all." Ryan stood up and unbuttoned his shirt. "I'm going for a swim. You coming?"

"No..... no I'll just lay here and watch." He noticed the change in Ryan's voice. He watched him splash in the Turkish bath-like water, though a strange sense of guilt hovered over him.

A moment passed by. An old bum ambled by, his mouth opened. Preston donated his tee shirt and stood up. His mind was running in a series of complexes. He strolled away along the beach and left Ryan in the distant water which seemed so remote. A flock of seagulls rose in the air screaming. Preston whirled around.

"I said, where you going?" Ryan's high pitched New Jersey accent was audible against the waves.

Preston dictated his okay sign. "To Peggy's home." Then he crossed the road and in his hurry bumped shoulders with a blonde haired woman who uttered a few harsh words.

Mr. Kennedy was conveying water from a flexible green tube over his broad lawn when Preston approached him. He was arrayed in a yellow flowered shirt and green pants. Preston removed his hands from his pockets and gazed at the white sumptuous house.

"Hi there," Mr. Kennedy shouted, "what can I do you for?"

His stout frame proceeded to lean on the amethyst Mercedes car and the water continued to fall on the sorghum grass.

"I'm looking for Peggy," Preston said. "Is she in right now?"

The shouts of pre-occupied children made palpitations arouse in Preston's heart as he gazed artlessly at the man who smiled, showing nicotine stained teeth.

"Well, you've come to the right place son." He motioned his hand to two green draped windows behind him. "Only she's kind of out right now with this tall....." He knitted his hirsute brows and looked above him at the blue expanse of sky, "... broad looking boy. Yeah, they left a few moments back."

Preston's eyes met his for a while. He was intrigued by the familiar face, but he wanted to turn now and go.

"Who might you be then?" the man smiled.

"Just a friend."

"Yeah, come to think of it, Peggy has a wide variety of friends." He followed Preston's gaze toward the rose bush where his elder daughter was clipping the buds. "Mainly boys though. Are you in her grade too?"

Preston spontaneously repressed the lump in his throat. "We're the same age, but she's more intelligent than me."

"That's weird you know, 'cause when I was a boy....."

Preston glanced peevishly up at the right window where he had previously been seeing the velvet drape twitch.

"We never had that kind of system." A figure momentarily disappeared from view.

Preston's eyes dropped to the oncoming girl, whose long brunette hair was dishevelled. She flashed a smile toward him and gently received the hose from her father's grasp.

"Take care of those roses now Lisa," the man yelled when the lean girl was a yard away. "Make sure you keep that hose angled to your left."

The girl, who looked about seventeen, turned, caught Preston's eye, surveyed him from head to toe, then gave a salacious smirk.

Preston turned to Mr. Kennedy who was now shining down the car with a white cloth. He appeared to be unaware of his presence now. Preston tapped his sneakers awkwardly; he shifted his hair from his eyes.

"How long has this boy known Peggy?" he asked.

The man continued his vigorous movements. "Well, like I said son, there's boys coming in here every day, they get to be tall or thin, fat or short, and I don't always remember them." He summarily stopped for breath and looked at Preston searchingly. "But I think I'll remember you though."

Preston experienced a sultry feeling over his face.

"The rest of them, they looked like J.D.'s. You don't. I get worried with Peggy, and the kids she chooses, they look as though they been down the joint more than once. Know what I mean?"

"Yeah, I know what you mean," said Preston, feeling the sun more intensive than usual around the back of his neck.

He had gone back to the beach and lay there until the stars in the inky sky revealed themselves. There was a big wind and the waves were driving up on his legs. Preston sauntered impulsively through the wet sand. Once or twice he glanced back at the sea and saw the dark water in resemblance of his desired pepsi cola. As if competing in a race Preston impelled his feet, and from the distant sea he thought he heard the echo of Ryan's voice.

"Where you going?" With great remorse he wondered why he had ever gone to Peggy's home at all.

In bed that night he could not sleep. He tried to erase Peggy from his mind. Eventually he got up and sat through the still night in the kitchen, drinking five cans of pepsi cola.

Tuesday afternoon Preston was walking home, drinking pepsi, his red checked shirt was open and the sweat streaked down his chest. A tall, faired-head girl, holding a book bag, sidled past him. She turned voluntarily, a haunting scent lingering, and Preston realised it was Peggy. Her face was dominated by a thoughtful expression. They walked together, then she suddenly stopped and stared at Preston.

"My dad had a visitor yesterday evening."

"I know, it was me."

Preston regarded her and a strange hollowness crept into his stomach.

"You oughtn't to visit me no more Preston." She slipped her hand to her hair in exasperation. "We're through, okay? Why don't you just leave me alone?"

Preston looked into her blue eyes. "What's with you Peg? Why are you going with Curt Miller?"

"That is no concern of yours." She retorted, "just..... I'd appreciate it if you don't come by again, okay?" She started to go.

"Wait Peggy." She gazed intolerantly at Preston. "I'm through with drinking pepsi, you know."

"So you're through, hey! I don't care anymore, right?" Her eyes drifted to Preston's hands, clasping two pepsi cola cans.

"C'mon, you don't really think I'm gonna believe that you dropped me 'cause I drink this stuff, do you?"

"Yeah."

"That's poison," Preston yelled.

"Like you."

He swept his eyes along the side walk.

"And how's your fairy friend Ryan Kassick doing? Okay, is he? I don't know what makes you hang in with him, he's a lousy creep."

"Just like Curt Miller."

"Yeah, just like Curt Miller, if that'll make you happy, but only far worse." She rounded the corner and Preston watched her move into the crowds. Her hair was the white waves of the foaming sea.

He went straight to his room, collapsed on his bed and listened to his palpitating heart, thinking it was audible to everybody. His mother came in a moment later. She ran her fingers through his hair: "You're getting more like your father every day, you know," she sighed. "He was just bone lazy and stubborn. Preston, is there anything the matter? Why'nt you tell me?..... That's what a mother's for you know, to help erase the problems on your mind." Silence. She got up from the bed and walked slowly to the door. "I'm gonna visit your father now, see you later, huh?" The door closed. Preston turned over and buried his face in the pillow.

When he awoke, his face felt strangely sore. The sun was going down and the apartment was filled with silence. Sitting on a white wicker chair in one corner of the room was Ryan. His eyes were large and earnest. He smiled. "Your sister told me you were sleeping, she let me come in."

Preston hesitated, then confused with sleep he lay back and gazed at the ceiling. "Is my sister still in?" he said, after a long while.

"She went out awhile back," came the reply. Ryan stood up and the wicker chair creaked.

"Well will you fetch me a can of pepsi. They're in the refrigerator."

"Would you rather have a cigarette Preston? I mean, I have lots."

"What, Marijuana? No thanks, hang on there, I'll get it myself." He glanced at his feet as they hit the blue carpet. "Hey, what're my feet doing like this?" Then he saw his white sneakers hanging on the door handle.

"I figured you looked uncomfortable in your sleep" Ryan said sheepishly, "so I kinda took 'em off."

"You're my friend for life, did you know that Ryan?" Preston smiled and he followed Ryan out of the room.

"Help yourself to a can." The refrigerator door slammed. "Are you hungry or anything? There's flapjacks yonder there Erica made."

"I'm not hungry Preston, I'm hot."

"Then turn the air conditioning down a little."

They went into the lounge. Preston slumped on the divan. Ryan collapsed beside him. "I'm hungry to do something, and I don't know what." Ryan ran his hand over his face.

"Like what, take a girl and have a good time in the sack?"

"No, something big." The room was silent. Preston gazed at his mother's wedding picture.

"Aaron wants to hit off a store again."

"And you too huh?" Preston gazed at him. "You and your brothers, it's rough all over. They like spending time down the joint?"

"Listen, what else is there to do? ....Life's one big headache." Ryan moved closer to Preston.

"Your mother's having a hard time keeping you out of trouble, Ryan."

"Hey, it ain't me. It's Aaron and Kip and Ashley, they're always pushing me into things like that."

Preston sipped his pepsi. "They're drop outs and you're not."

"But I'm figuring on dropping out of that school too, Preston. It's a drag, know what I mean?" He grinned. Preston sipped his pepsi. "Besides, I'm not cut out for that kind of lousy work that Miss Rosenberg fills my head with. I'm all for raiding stores, getting high, and having myself a great time."

"Me too," Preston got up.

"Where you going?"

"Only to get another pepsi."

When he came back Ryan was recumbent on the divan. Preston lay on the white carpet beneath him and swallowed his pepsi carefully. The room was silent, apart from a ticking dime store clock.

"Hey, where do you hussle all the dough from to buy all 'em drinks Preston?" Ryan asked a while later.

"I don't pilfer them. I had me an evening job once."

"What I mean is that you could have yourself a whole load of 'em in no time."

"You mean like, hold up a store. Right?"

"Now you're talking." Ryan sat up and looked down at Preston. "we could do it at night, while nobody's around. We could bust in."

"Hey, what? Just the two of us?"

"I'll be hanged if we do. No, my brothers will help too."

"Why? Why when July 4th's coming up?" Preston sat up.

"We could do it weeks before that."

Preston shook his head. "I don't know. I don't think so Ryan." He was thinking of Peggy. He remembered her father's words.

Ryan's eyes were penetrating as he moved to get up. With a quick jerk, Ryan was on top of him. Preston could feel his wet hands on his back, over his stomach, and the tickling made him give way to laughter.

"C'mon Preston, say you'll do it," he urged. He remained on top of him and Preston felt a curious sensation run up his spine. He stopped laughing. Ryan's hand was touching his chest and caressing it gently. "Say you'll raid the store with me."

His breath on Preston's skin was like the breeze of a wind. He felt his skin go warm and cold all over. Preston lay still, looking into his eyes. They were remote and happy.

An apprehension seized him. "Hey Ryan, what's the difference between a cemetery and a john?" Ryan did not respond. "When you gotta go you gotta go." He heaved himself strenuously away and slid out of his grasp.

"Will you raid the store with me Preston?"

"Yes Ryan." Preston ran out the room. He was suddenly glad to be away from him, and a perplexing sensation was with him, but he didn't know why.

A week drifted by. The light of the sun was fading into an overall gloom. Preston was sedentary, his chin in his hands, two empty pepsi cola cans lay at his feet; a third beside him on the table, half empty.

His sister had been creating a clamour in her room for a long while. Preston sipped his pepsi and thought: she must be going out again. But he could not detect the usual spray of her perfume. He thought: she must be getting ready for bed. A moment later, with an audible shriek, a door opened hitting the wall sending reverberations throughout the apartment. In a second Preston jolted up to see Erica coming toward him. In her face was an aspect of extreme malice.

"Preston, so God help you. I'm gonna hang you when I catch you."

Nonplussed, Preston eyed his sister suspiciously as she flounced up to him knocking the pepsi cola can out of his hand. She grabbed his shoulders and proceeded to drag him up. "Hey," he yelled "wait a moment."

He struggled as Erica roughly pushed him.

"You just get inside my bedroom and tell me a few things, okay?"

"What the hell are you on about?"

A sharp slap on his face followed his attempt to escape. "Hey, quit that."

Erica, a little taller than him, commenced to propel him up the grey carpeted corridor. He stumbled only to receive an excruciating stab in the back. Erica's nail felt like a razor sharp blade. He ineffectually tried to suppress a cry. Once in the room Erica slammed the door shut.

"I warned you about going into my room."

"Hey, I didn't even go in your room."

"Quit lying Preston." She grabbed his hair. "Who'd you take me for, some crazy bred nut?"

"What's the matter?"

"I'll tell you what's the matter." She pulled him down sideways until his face was level with the second drawer. "There's something missing from inside that."

"So what? You don't have to blame it on me."

"Well who else do I blame it on? Look into this drawer Preston and you tell me what's goddammed missing."

Preston, his face taut, a numbness growing in his head peeked stupidly from bleary eyes and saw an assortment of hazy colours. Black, blue, yellow, red, green; he could not detect his sister's meaning. He looked up at the polka dot ceiling.

"I don't miss anything."

"Say that again." Preston closed his eyes as she pinched his cheek.

"Five dollars is a hell of a lot of money, and I didn't just save it up to have it hussled by my brother. You know that?" She let go the grip on his hair, scrutinised him as he recoiled and lost his balance, collapsing on the pink patchwork covered bed. "I didn't take nothing, hear?"

"I hear," Erica shouted through clenched teeth. "But if you think I'm gonna make believe that my money just happened to walk outta here when I've got such perfect reason to know it's you, then you can think again." She flounced towards him, yanked him up and repeatedly, with viciousness, plunked him on each side of his head.

"Hey...... stop...."

"C'mon, tell me what you done with my money? What'd you spend it on? Sex mags huh? Funkey music? Pepsi cola? Weeds? Or did you spend it on your girl friends?...."

Preston, seeing stars, his hearing confused, lay back helplessly, his hands pinioned down by his sister's strength. "You know, if I did buy all those things you said, I bought them with my own money."

Preston challenged his sister's cold stare and thought, she doesn't trust me. With a jerk he recovered his strength, forced her arms up and manipulated them as they flew at his face in frenzy.

"You're not going anywheres."

He was up from the bed. Feeling a hand round his waist he lashed out and fought off his opposition with a professional bound from her grasp. Zipping down the corridor like a streak of lightning, Preston collided with the front door, which he swung open. His heart was pounding as he suddenly stopped in front of a tawny-haired woman. His mother looked perplexed. "Well what on God's green earth..... what the hell are you running from? The devil?"

"I am too." Preston touched his sore head. For once in his life he was glad to see her.

"Yeah." Shouted Erica, flailing herself toward them. "Momma, would you just look at him?" Preston dodged her arm.

"Yeah, I'm looking at him honey." Mrs. Wildey-King stepped into the apartment, her eyes on Preston. "All I can see is a...."

"What you're looking at there is a double-crossing lying thief." Erica's eyes were blazing as she attempted to prod Preston. "Momma I just did my nut saving that five dollars and now my own brother has taken it!" She looked pleadingly at her mother. "If you don't do something...... dammit Preston, it's all those lousy, rotten, crazy cans of pepsi cola, that you buy every day of your life, with my money."

She flounced to the refrigerator, opened it and impetuously lifted out four cans, smashing them to the floor. Ripping out another can, the liquid poured on the floor.

Preston, with anger rising, knocked the table in full force and flew to his sister's side. She pummelled him with cans and screamed loudly, as she felt her arm twisted. "Let go."

"Preston, leave go of your sister this moment, and Erica, I know what I'm about to do you if you don't clean that mess up," yelled Mrs. Wildey-King sternly.

"They're going in the trash can once'n for all," screeched Erica. She pushed past her mother, her arms full of cans, and disappeared, the clamour of cans rolling down the steps.

"You didn't take the money, did you Preston?" said Mrs. Wildey-King firmly.

"I didn't take the money."

She sat down, her chin in her hands. Preston was feeling hurt, physically and emotionally. His head went dizzy. He eyed his mother, then his heart jumped.

"Why'd I have to have a brother who's a lousy pepsi cola addict?" Erica demanded as she flounced into the room again. "Why, why, why?" Her hand flew to her head. "Preston, I'm asking you a damn question, a question is a question, and it won't be one without an answer, did you take my money?'

A shadow passed Preston's face; his arms dropped stiffly to his sides.

"Answer your sister Preston, before I have one of my migraines."

"Did you?"

"No I did not, now shuddup," he yelled, grabbing a chair, swinging it around and attempting to throw it. Mrs. Wildey-King quickly stubbed out her cigarette, lunged forward, and tugged the chair. "Oh no you don't, not in my kitchen."

Preston let go. Blindly he picked up a plate, and hurled it directly at Erica, who dodged as the sound of smashing echoed through the sombre apartment. A short silence.

"Look what you've done to my china." Preston flinched as his mother plunked his head. He charged forward, and Erica caught his arm. "You hussled my money." Preston attacked her with his fist, and felt the pain in his knuckles along with the crack of her mouth. Charging through the open door, hearing the anguished cry of his sister, Preston ignored the frantic shouts of his mother. Taking two pepsi colas he rounded the corner with a feeling of persecution.

The squalid house, surrounded by mosquito-plagued trash cans was a relief to Preston as he reached it. Four pairs of blue overalls were suspended on a washing line, and the sound of a lawn mower made a nostalgic home coming.

"I seen you coming," Ryan announced as he swung back the screen door.

"Hey babe, what's bugging you?" he had a questioning look in his eyes.

Preston smiled sadly.

"You look beat! Hey, who made you up like this, huh?" Ryan touched Preston's temple.

"Yah, black 'n blue all over," Aaron intervened from behind his brother. "hey boy, you better come in."

"Hey, do I look that bad?"

"More than that." Aaron took hold of his arm, and steered him into a stuffy room. Preston winced as he eyed his reflection in a dusty mirror. Swelling bruises dominated his left cheek and his face seemed flushed. One side of his head was prominent; as he touched it a sharp pain shot through his head.

"Who beat you, Peggy?" Ryan joked.

"My sister." A ripple of laughter filled the room.

"No, not Miss Independence again, she's always beating you." exclaimed Ashley. "Hey, you beat her back next time." He smacked his hands together and tossed his dark mane of hair. "Ask her to date me will you, and boy am I liable to cool her down a little."

"She'd most probably bite your head off." Preston rubbed his face and licked his dry lips. The lawn mower had stopped.

"Hey, I hope she ain't like that in bed, otherwise she's gonna wind up one of a hell of a different girl by the time

I'm through with her," Ashley retorted. Another burst of laughter vibrated round the room.

"What'd she hit you for?" Ryan asked. His eyes were translucent in the sunset.

"I hit her back too, she accused me of pilfering her money. She's a pain in the ass."

"How much Preston?" Aaron whispered. "You didn't take none, did you?"

"I'm not a thief Aaron. I'm a pepsi cola addict. Two different things. Right." Preston felt a cold uneasiness run up his back. There was a short silence. He glanced around the suffocating room. Blankly it stared back at him.

"Shoot Preston." Ashley put his arm around his shoulder. "Me and you got the same feelings, nobody gonna tell us to cry for the moon, when we want to cry for the sun, right?" He ruffled his hair and Preston's head felt like a cannon ball about to go off.

They sat around the pine-wood table. A savoury aroma invaded the room. They made big shadows on the shabby wall.

"You sure you won't eat some pizza?" Aaron insisted. He pushed the plate around to Preston.

"I'm not hungry."

"How about some cole slaw?" Kip invited.

Preston wearily eyed the tall muscular brothers of Ryan and sipped his pepsi cola. "No thanks."

He felt an arm around his shoulder at that moment. "Are you still for raiding that store with us Preston?" Ryan asked.

"I'm all for doing anything you like."

The door squeaked open, and a sparse, sour-looking woman came over to the lamplight. "You ain't gonna be needing this now, boys." Her eyes swept over to Preston. "And who might you be?"

"Aw mom, he's a friend and he's staying the night. Now would you give us back the light please?"

"Ashley, we're trying to save the fuel, you'll sit in darkness or you'll get out the house, whichever way you choose, this lamp ain't burning tonight."

"Aw hell, I'm going to bed, and I'm finding me a job in the morning. I can't stick this no more." Ashley brought his hand down hard on the table and stood up.

"I'll slap your face for you, hear, if you break them plates." The woman proceeded to blow out the lamp. "You're only sixteen years and already you think you can own the world." The door closed slowly and the room was enveloped in a hazy darkness. Sparks of red sunlight peeked in at the miserable windows. To Preston, surveying the room, it seemed complete tranquillity. For some unknown reason, he wistfully wanted to remain sitting there all night.

"You can sleep in your clothes," Ryan whispered a few hours later.

Ashley was recumbent on his bed, nearby was Aaron. Kip was standing before the dresser, yawning. The roof of the bedroom was slanted downwards; it gave the atmosphere a diminished and untidy look.

Preston thought about his own room. His own bed. He stretched up, yanked off his red-blocked striped tee shirt and lay on the soft bed beside Ryan. A moment later he was thinking of Peggy. Peggy running her hands through his hair, soothing the pain in his head. Peggy lying beside him, instead of Ryan. Then he saw Curt Miller standing, virile, beside her and the pain in his head increased. He wanted a drink of pepsi but he couldn't move, so he lay there listening to the waves of the sea and softly cried himself to sleep.

In the morning, he opened his eyes, his head like a log and Ryan's arm across his chest. He lay there for a while, until he remembered where he was and what had happened. He sat up quickly. Aaron, Ashley and Kip had gone.

"Where you going?" Ryan's voice was sleepy. He stirred and sat up, his hair tousled.

"To the can, it's morning, I gotta get home." His voice sounded artificial to his ears. Ryan placed a warm hand on his shoulder.

"I never heard you cry like that before. Preston, you were talking in your sleep too. What's the matter?"

Preston lay back as though he had been hit and gazed up at the dingy ceiling. "From the day I was born, Ryan, to now and the seconds in between, my life has been one big shipwreck. I don't think I can take it any longer."

Ryan stared at him dolefully. "Hey, you should never have got on that ship, you know that?"

"That's not what I mean," Preston replied feebly. "I'm figuring on bumping myself off."

"That's the easy way out Preston, and as the Indians say, any time's as good as today to die."

Preston glanced dazedly at Ryan. There followed a short silence, in which a dying radio murmured out its last breath of music; the sounds of voices; a door slamming.

"But I guess it ain't easy for human beings, and that means us too." Ryan stared hard at Preston. Sometimes his eyes wandered. "Every guy's gotta make a mistake some time in their lives. That I guess, is one thing we gotta accept as human beings."

"I don't know. I don't think I'm even a human any more."

"What are you then, a freak? Or don't you even know you're an adolescent? Hey we're going through a weird time." Ryan's voice was dreamy. "It's like a kind of challenge. Know what I mean?"

Preston pressed the side of his head. He wanted the pain to increase.

"It takes courage I guess." Ryan said. "Right now I can see a hazy road in front of me. It has plenty of rough spots too."

"That's why I'm a failure," Preston murmured, "and I guess I always will be."

Ryan rested on his elbows, the sun shining on his face. "You know, once I thought I would die, but I didn't, and I just went around in a dream for days."

"Why'd you wanna die?"

Ryan shifted his hair from his eyes. "Because it was the time my father left us and I was just a kid. The going was hard."

Preston had a desperate feeling rising faster in his mind. For a moment he imagined god staring down at him. He was shaking his finger. Preston shook his head. "What made you live?"

"I was eight and afraid of death." Ryan swung his legs over the bed.

Preston looked at him. His face carried deep remorse. "Are you still afraid? You know, of death?"

"Yes and no, and hey, let's quit this talk, okay?"

"Okay," replied Preston, and taking his tee shirt he ambled out the room.

When he opened the door to the apartment, an aroma of coffee and pancakes drifted toward him. He closed the door quietly. His sister who was attending the stove, turned around clad in white bath robe, towel wrapped around her head and a dark, wet curl plastered to her forehead. Preston noticed her face. Her lower lip revealed a cut. It was swollen and made one side of her lips enlarged. Preston felt a feeling of guilt. He stared at his sister, who stared back wide eyed with a peculiar expression on her refreshed face.

"Well hi there, Prezzie," she said, surprised, "how's life? Okay?"

Preston shrugged his shoulders. "Okay."

"Thought you weren't coming back, but you left your bags behind." She turned to the sizzling pancakes, flapped then over and glanced at Preston, still motionless by the door.

"Well what's the matter, you glued to the door?"

"Where's mom?"

"In her room going wild 'bout you, you're gonna catch it you know." The windows were steamed up. Over by the faucets a single drop of water dripped.

"I've only been to Ryan's house."

Erica proceeded to lay some cutlery and plates on the table. "Listen, I'm fixing pancakes. You eaten yet?"

Preston gazed at his sister morbidly then turned to the corridor. "I don't eat breakfast."

A door opened. Mrs. Wildey-King, in checked pants, her hair freshly brushed, appeared. "Preston, that you?" On seeing her son, an expression of relief dominated her face. It did not match Preston's earlier picture. She spontaneously kissed and hugged him. "Hey, where've you been? Looks to me as if you've just climbed out your grave."

"I don't know. Around and about."

A piece of cutlery clanged to the floor. "Thought you said you been to Ryan's house," Erica interrupted.

Preston swung round. "So. Ryan's house, what's the difference, huh?"

His mother pulled his tee shirt. "Don't get worked up again, okay?" she whispered. "I don't like it when you hassle with your sister like that."

"Hey, she hassled me. You know that too." Preston stood back.

"And you know I can't stand that."

"She's always kicking up some kind of fuss."

His mother tapped his shoulder. He flinched. "Just take it easy, okay? And put a band aid on that cut."

He went to his room taking off his tee shirt slowly. A moment later, a towel on his shoulder, he stopped in the corridor on his way to the bathroom and listened to his sister's voice.

"What's with him huh? He goes round as though his head was up in the clouds.… stumbling off a cliff.…"

Preston pulled the towel tightly round his neck. He closed the door.

He was standing in front of the mirror combing his wet hair, and inspecting his bruises when the door opened.

"Hey, do I come into your room when you're undressing?" Preston's complaint rose to anger when he saw her in the mirror. He turned round sharply.

"That depends on what kind of boy you are," Erica replied, closing the door. "I came by to tell you about that five dollars."

"To hell with it." Preston faced the mirror, continuing light strokes with the comb on his hair.

"I guess I was wrong to blame it on you, I know that now too. My mind goes blank sometimes. I spent it last week."

Preston swallowed hard. Water from his hair trickled down to his nose. He wiped it impatiently.

"Listen, you don't have to give me the pass up."

Preston put the comb down, pushing the hair from his eyes.

"I'm sorry I hit you so."

Preston clenched his jaws. "Then get out before I make you real sorry you did." He turned around.

Erica opened the door. "Look what you've done to my lip. Now how in hell am I gonna kiss my boyfriends, huh?"

"That ain't my problem."

"It is too, you rotten lousy, low down, stumblebum." Erica slammed the door, sending sensations of numbness through Preston's ears.

When he awoke sometime later, his heart was palpitating. His hair was still wet, so he thought he must be sweating. He was cold, a feeling that always visited him whenever he slept during daytime. He was in need of his pepsi cola. I'm too weak to get one, he thought wistfully. There was the sound of heavy breathing.

He outlined the side of the can with a little modern art. Mrs. Rosenberg came up behind him, pencil in her mouth. "Hey that's swell Preston. I never knew you had such good drawing abilities. How about inscribing the name of the drink as well on the can." The paper flapped slightly with the cool afternoon breeze, which breathed provocatively through the opened windows. "What is it? .... pepsi?"

"Yeah, pepsi cola." As she ambled away among the occupied students, Preston found himself licking his lips thirstily. A summer silence drifted by.

"Hey, Preston where you going?" Mrs. Rosenberg whirled around.

"To the bathroom." She shook her small head, perplexed.

"Have you a weak bladder or something? You're always going to the bathroom, you know that?"

A few girls collecting more paints from a side table laughed loudly. Preston's face changed. Eyes down, he winced and slipped out the door.

"I said, stop laughing." He heard the teacher's thin, austere voice ring throughout the echoing building.

Preston's sneakers squeaked rhythmically, as he swaggered his way through the shiny corridor. Two coloured boys, clad in basket ball gear, perspiration running down their faces, bounced past him. Their loud talk was audible as Preston came to the end of the corridor. He passed the bathroom and turned into the locker room. Digging out the key from his pocket, he opened the steel cupboard. Behind the pair of sleeping sneakers was one solitary pepsi cola. He opened it abruptly and drank, his thoughts drowned in the cold drink.

He glanced on the grey wall. The clock read half of two. Shrugging his shoulders, he closed the locker and headed toward the swing door, quickening his pace as he neared the entrance of the building.

"Hey, King, is that you?"

Preston instantly recognised the janitor's voice. Without glancing back he increased his running. The sun scorched him, a feeling of freedom came over him as he raced through the campus, slowing his footsteps as he neared the intersection. Preston licked the running liquid off his hand, and downed the remains of the can. He walked home slowly.

He pushed the apartment door open, and closed it firmly behind him.

"What are you doing home?" his mother said, raising her eye brows, as she came out of the kitchen.

"What're you doing home mom?" He hung his denim jacket on the coat stall.

"You feeling okay, Preston?"

"I'm feeling fine. How about you?"

Mrs. Wildey-King smiled. "Fine, fine. Listen I'm having coffee with a friend in the kitchen, okay? Don't hesitate if you want something." She looked anxiously at Preston for a while then went back down the corridor, closing the door behind her.

An hour later Preston came out of his room. Erica was standing gangling and chatting to the telephone. He sidled past her and slipped through the door, taking his jacket. When he reached the arcade he ambled toward Bennison's store. He pushed the transparent door open. A girl with a heart-shaped face and pointed chin, was serving a customer. She glanced up and smiled.

Preston fingered the drink shelf absently. He was gazing at the liquor bottles marked Vodka, when a hand turned him around.

"What you want kid, we don't sell fire water to kids under sixteen, understand?" His eyes met a man's windblown face, with an austere light in his eyes.

Preston felt a warmness creep up his back. Apprehensively he felt the whole store had eyes on him. "Listen, I'm buying pepsi cola, okay?"

The man moved away. When Preston glanced around again he saw that the girl, free of customers, was gazing somewhat lasciviously at him. He took three cans of pepsi and walked directly toward her. She looked about twenty; her large blue eyes seemed prominent from the rest of her face. Her white pinafore dress strained across her breasts as she turned to calculate money on the large till.

Preston glanced at her hands. Finding no ring on her finger, he looked closer at her. She looked back at him.

"That'll be one dollar, two nickels please." Feeling the touch of her hand as he handed her the money, Preston felt a quiver pass through him. He looked intently into her eyes, his excited passion aroused as he sensed a new look come about her. Immediately a hardening pain hit him between his eyes. Preston detached himself from his trance. Hot, speechless he turned and went through the open door, carrying his cans awkwardly.

Reaching the distant pay phone, alongside the extravagant movie house, where girls and boys congregated noisily, Preston closed the door behind him. Picking up the phone, his drinks already trickling down his throat, he pushed the dime in and dialled Peggy's number, 5705. He waited patiently to the prolonged purring sound. It stopped abruptly as the receiver was picked up.

"Hello?"

"Hello." replied a subdued voice. "Who is this please?"

Preston had a sudden picture of a small woman with a tense face. He thought that she could already see him. He crimsoned, his armpits drenching his tee shirt. "I'm a friend of Peggy's. Is she in please?" There was a pause, and the sound of crackling. Preston eyed the girl in the cream dress, through the glass pane. The boy in the Stetson was pushing and grabbing at her roughly.

For a moment his mind swayed. The boy pushed the girl to the wall.... they embraced, their hands roaming....

"Yes, she's in, but she's kind of busy right now." Preston jumped back to reality.

"Um.... listen I'd just like to talk to her." He drummed his fingers on the mouthpiece. There was a pause.

"She's catching up on some work, but I guess I'll go ask her if she'd like to talk to you."

A moment later, which seemed like an hour, Preston recognised Peggy's voice as it met his ears.

"Hi.... who is this huh?"

Preston swallowed. His heart was beating too loud; maybe she could hear. "It's.... Preston Wildey-King here and...."

"Whaddya want with me?" There was sudden anger in her voice.

"Peggy, let's talk awhile, okay? But not like this."

"Why not?" There was a silence. "Say what you have to, Preston, right here on this phone. There's...."

"I can't, babe," Preston clicked his tongue, "I have to see you.... now."

Peggy sounded as though she had drawn in her breath. "Listen.... I don't understand you Preston, but I think I know the way you feel about me."

"Babe, I happen to love you." Preston's hands were shaking. He tried to restrain himself from the exciting thoughts that were mounting inside his head.

"Don't say that Preston..... I won't see you tonight. Maybe I'll see you tomorrow."

"Don't give me that."

"I already have." The phone clicked and a dead whirring sound reached Preston's ears. He was thinking he was mad. He was thinking maybe he was going to cry. Slamming down and then picking the receiver up, he pushed in another dime. The phone on the other side was picked up immediately.

"Hey Peggy, don't do this to me."

"Hey Preston, how come I always get to do something to you.... have you realised what you're doing to me?"

Preston squeezed his eyes shut.

"I'll see you tomorrow down on the beach. 2 o'clock and not before that."

"Yeah, and I'm figuring you're having a great time in bed with that Curt Miller. He's a sucker."

The phone went dead.

Dejected, he pushed the door open and blindly ambled across the street. Why do I buy time with her, he thought, I'm going crazy about her. She won't even appreciate the fact that I love her......

"Hey Preston." He whirled around impetuously. Ashley Kassick was headed his way, head down, long hair flowing. "Hey you coming to the movies?"

Preston shrugged his shoulders. "What's on?"

"'Moment by Moment' with John Travolta. It sounds pretty good." He turned to glance back at the crowd on the other side. "There's Dee-Dee, now she's a real little number."

Preston followed his arm to a tall slender brunette, standing solitary with high stilettos and a polka dot dress. "She's swell, and I think she digs me too."

Preston swept his eyes to the ground. "I don't think so."

Ashley was silent for a moment as he looked back at the girl. "You don't think what?"

"I don't think I'll come to the movies, right?"

"Okay Preston." He punched him lightly on the shoulder. "And hey, Ryan says he'll come by tomorrow sometime."

Preston looked up. He watched him amble back to Dee-Dee. He thought, that's me and that's Peggy and we're happy..... at last.

They were on the beach. Peggy threw pebbles into the sea. Preston scrutinised her yellow clinging tee shirt with amorous eyes. A burning sensation reached his neck and he knew it was not the sun.

"What you said on the phone yesterday Preston, I believed you."

"What, that I love you?" He unbuttoned his check shirt, taking it off slowly.

Peggy looked at him; she stopped throwing pebbles. "Do you? I mean do you for one moment think that what you're saying is true?"

He shrugged his shoulders, and laughed timidly. "You know I do Peggy. Why all these dumb questions? Why play all these dumb games?"

"I'm not playing dumb games." The water flapped like a bird in the air.

"Then what, huh?"

"Don't snow me Preston."

"Then what? C'mon what am I supposed to do, sit on my ass all day? Wait around till you feel you can face me, after you've been sleeping in with Curt Miller?"

Peggy dropped her eyes. "Shuddap."

"No. Who do you take me for, I'm no one night stand. I'm not like the guys you hang in with, okay?"

The birds laughed, as they circled in the air. The waves whispered back angrily.

"What difference does that make? Maybe you're the best thing since blueberry muffins. Maybe you're just a pepsi cola freak. What do I care, huh?" Her eyes blazed as Preston took her arm.

"Hey don't say that. You know who I am."

"Oh quit that talk and grow up."

"Hey listen." Preston flung her arm away. "Don't tell me to grow up, Peggy, when you're the one that needs to." He turned away. There was a forlorn silence as they both gazed out to sea. Peggy hunched her shoulders, crossed her arms as she stared at Preston. Her eyes held a stern look. "You don't have to be so fresh."

Preston, lost in his thoughts, drew a deep breath and shivered under the hot sun. "Peggy you really got it made, you know that?"

She gave a sarcastic laugh. "Hey, that's funny."

"No, to hell it's not funny." Preston swung around, his eyes hard on Peggy as she crimsoned slightly. For a moment they stared at each other; grave; solemn; serious. Preston thought, she's not looking at me, she's testing me.

"Hey, that's something." Her lips curled intentionally.

"Yeah, and I'm a million laughs." His face changed as he listened to his beating heart. "You make believe everything's right, Peggy, when to hell it's not."

"You can stop being so damn proud of yourself," Peggy snapped.

"Hey, look who's talking. I'm proud? Alright, c'mon you tell me what I've got to be proud of..... tell me." Preston hit his chest. "Tell me..... right you don't know, then don't you ever again try telling me what I'm proud of, when I don't even know what that is, okay?"

Peggy turned away. There was a tense pause. A breeze disturbed the warm air. A man in Bermuda shorts stole past them. His eyes displayed amusement as he stared back.

"You didn't have to shout so loud, Preston."

"Hey I could tell the whole world, if I wanted to."

"Tell the whole world what?"

"About us and our crazy way of life."

"Big deal," Peggy retorted, exasperated. "Don't you mean your life, your crazy way of phoning girls up who are already through with you?"

Preston strained his eyes across the sea, then up the beach, feeling deflated. "Hey, listen, I didn't come here to fight with you Peg."

She tossed her hair rapidly. "Then what? Why did you come here? Why'd you phone me? To make nice with each other?" Her eyes showed sudden triumph. "Well, you've ruined that chance Preston." She turned abruptly and proceeded to walk away.

Preston counted her steps, then quickened his pace too. "Hey wait Peggy, I wanna ask you something."

She stopped a distance away, then turned sharply and began to walk rapidly back. "Ask me what? Do I still love you? Do you still love me? You don't even know whether you do or not. You're just waiting for me to answer your damn questions 'cause you don't know how to yourself. Isn't that right, Preston?" She was out of breath. Her voice came in short screams. "Well, don't you even try to ask me any more questions, 'cause if you do you're only gonna get the same reply, and that is NO."

Preston's eyes were beginning to sting; he clenched his jaws to hold on to the muscles of his face. For a moment he could only focus on Peggy's mystified face, then he turned, the glaze breaking, his eyes clearing as the tears at last rolled freely down his face.

He walked on rapidly until he knew that Peggy was nowhere in sight, then he stopped, trying to restrain his tears, and stared out at the sea which whispered his sadness with him.

Preston had an erotic dream that night. He dreamed he was having coition with Peggy on the beach. It was cold and dark when he glanced at her again he saw it was Ryan. His eyes were large and shining. Preston woke up in a cold sweat. His hands were clutched tightly to his pillow, somewhere in the inky darkness he thought he saw a shadow glide past. He thought it was his father coming to tuck him up. For a while he lay awake with a feeling that he wanted to remember something.... Something that drew a blank picture across his mind.

He fell asleep exhausted, and when the morning came his head was mixed with emotions.

He ambled toward the refrigerator and had just taken one sip of his pepsi cola, when the door bell rang. It was Ryan and his face held a somewhat sentimental expression. Preston gazed at him hard; he was afraid to let his eyes fall, and again that urgent sensation that he had to remember something came flying back to him.

He saw that Ryan's eyes were searching his. "What's the matter Preston?"

"Nothing." He intensified his stare. "How come you always get to think something's the matter with me?"

Ryan shrugged, raising his eyebrows, and stepped in. "I came by yesterday and you were out someplace."

"I was on the beach...... with Peggy."

Ryan's face changed. "How come you walked outta school on Friday?"

"I didn't walk, I ran." Preston attempted a laugh. "Besides I was thirsty. Hey, did anybody miss me?"

"About half the school, and they thought I was kidding when I told 'em you were a desperate pepsi cola addict."

"Come in the den." Preston said reluctantly. "Switch on the tube. Put some music on. I'm taking a shower."

Quarter of an hour later, with a towel wrapped around his waist, Preston went into the lounge. He was anxious to know why Ryan had called. There was a cacophony of music coming from the mahogany stereogram. Ryan was reclining on the divan listlessly and smoking a cigarette.

"Hey Ryan, did you call me?" Preston rubbed his damp chest.

Ryan sat up and looked at him. "No I didn't call you. You thought I did?"

"Yeah, it sounded like you." For a moment Ryan stared at him.

"Hey, you shouldn't be walking around the place like that!"

"Why not?" Preston felt a pang of irritation.

"Because you're liable to catch your death, and besides somebody could be spying on you."

"Hey, it happens to be the middle of summer, and nobody's spying at me through the windows."

"How'd you know?"

"'Cause I know so. Hey, close those drapes." Ryan reached laboriously to the sable drapes. Preston switched the television on and collapsed on the divan.

"Hey babe, whaddya think you're doing, you can't watch the tube while I'm listening to music."

Preston remained motionless. "And why not? I can watch T.V. if I want to, you know."

"Yeah but...."

"Hey, what's eating you Preston?" The crescendo of music died away, as Ryan turned off the record. For a while the room was filled with a forced silence. "Shall I stack the records back on the shelf?"

Preston nodded his head once. "And hey, watch your cigarette. I don't want holes in the divan, my mom'll kill me."

A relaxing moment engaged the room, like a relief from a ringing phone. Ryan flounced down beside Preston. "What's on the tube?"

It broke a thought from Preston's mind. "You have eyes don't you?"

"What you blind, or what? Of course I have eyes."

Preston stared hard at the television; his eyes slipped to Ryan. He had a burning sensation. He could feel Ryan's eyes piercing inside him. He kept his eyes fixed on the show. "Hey Ryan, would you quit looking at me like that."

A haze of smoke rose in the air. "Who said anything about looking?"

Preston turned. "I did, and I didn't like it."

"I have eyes, don't I." Ryan stubbed out his cigarette on a nearby ash tray.

"You have eyes all right." Preston shook his head, confused. "You got the wrong kind. You're always staring at me like..... like I don't know."

Ryan's face crimsoned quickly. "Hey, everybody's gotta stare sometime."

"You don't. You stare all the time, like as if I were some kind of goddam freak."

Ryan looked away.

"If you wanna look at somebody, look at Erica, look at Peggy. They're the kind you should be looking at, not me."

"Maybe I like you better."

Preston felt his heart jump. "Hey Ryan, don't say that."

"I've already said it..... babe." Ryan's eyes enlarged radiantly.

"Well you've said it once," Preston yelled, seizing him by his sweatshirt, "but you're not gonna say it again, and quit calling me babe."

Ryan smirked. "Right babe, I won't call you babe anymore. I'm only saying that to turn you on."

Preston let go his hold. A hot sensation ran down his back. "What'd you say?"

"Hey Preston, can't you even take a joke?"

"No, and don't say that again."

Ryan glanced up at the ceiling. "Right."

"And it better be right or God so help me, I'll break every bone that you own. I mean that Ryan."

"Yeah."

"Yeah, well I'm gonna get dressed now." He rose from the divan. Half way across the room he turned sharply. He stared at Ryan. Ryan folded his arms and stared back, a strange light in his eyes.

"You want me to leave, Preston?"

"I don't care," he shrugged.

"Don't you really care?"

"Why should I care, huh?"

"I thought you were my friend?"

"So, I'm your friend. What about it? You want me to come over there to you and kiss you?"

Ryan looked away annoyed. "That ain't what I mean." Apart from the television show, the atmosphere was tense.

"Then what do you mean?" Preston ambled back to the divan. "Don't you mean it that way? Don't you want me to lean over now and kiss you?"

"Preston, quit that talk."

"Preston quit that talk," he mimicked. "No, why should I? Who started it? My best buddy started it, and you know why? He's a fairy, that's why. Yeah I heard the rumour all around town. I'm not that dumb."

Ryan got up impetuously, his face contorted in rage, in pain. He advanced to Preston with his fists raised.

Preston recoiled. "Hey don't you even touch me or I'll stamp out your brains."

Ryan stopped short. The muscles of his face were trembling. In his eyes was an ensnared, sensual look. Preston was thinking, he looks like a wild animal. He broke out in a clammy sweat. His feet seemed suddenly rooted to the ground. What's happening to me? His heart beat painfully as he watched Ryan approach him. His face stung when Ryan slowly touched it, continued down his arm, across his chest, as Ryan caressed him.

"You wouldn't really like to stamp out my brains...... now would you baby?"

Preston turned his face away. It was immediately forced back.

"Look at me Preston. Can't you see that I'm passionately in love with you?"

Preston had no time to think. He felt a sensational vibration around his waist. Like a slow motion picture, he watched his towel fall to the ground. Ryan's lips were between his legs, kissing, caressing, so that it made his whole body erect.

"Oh, God, you must've been created out of heaven. You are..... beautiful," Ryan whispered breathlessly. "You are..... a wonderful creation of work."

Preston shook his head, blinked his eyes. He pressed his cold hands down on Ryan's head. "Cut this out..... hey Ryan....."

"Be quiet." His voice was calm. "I'm gonna make you feel like you never felt before. I'm gonna make sure you never look at a girl the same way again."

A surge of apprehension seized Preston. He could not move. He would not move. Ryan's hands were spreading all over his body, wet lips brushed his chest, his nipples. He went hot, cold. I wanna scream he thought. Why..... why me God?

"Oh Christ," Ryan yelled emotionally, "I love you more than anything else in the world. I wanna be with you all the time."

Preston tried to control his quivering lips. "Hey Ryan, don't do this to me. Hell, I don't wanna be known as some freak."

Slowly Ryan rose. His breath warm, he put his arm around Preston's neck, leaning his head on his shoulder. "Hey, kid, I'm sorry. I didn't mean it to go this far. There was this guy with this beautiful face and this great body and these gorgeous eyes. It was you, and Preston you have the most wonderful manner..... you're..... just beautiful."

For a moment they stood swaying..... Preston went cold. He smelled Ryan's hair, he touched it. The world came crashing back to him. Slowly his senses crept back. Suddenly he grabbed hold of Ryan's wrists, and strenuously pushed him off. Ryan fell back on the floor. Preston snatched his towel up, walking toward him, and struck him heavily across the face. "Get out of my house, you lousy son of a bitch and don't come back."

Ryan struggled to his feet, eyes wide and watering as Preston continued the blows to his face, head and chest. As Ryan fell again, Preston had a strange desire to kill him.... wanted to kill his best friend. His mind was in complete turmoil, his anger up to his brains. "Now get up, I said, and get out."

He grabbed hold of Ryan's shoulders, and tried to haul him across the room. The coffee table rolled over, his mother's wedding picture fell to the floor, and it cracked loudly under the weight of Ryan. In another moment Preston lost control of his hands; he punched, scratched, and tore at Ryan's hair.

"Hey Preston," Ryan screamed, "look we can still be friends."

Preston stared at him, his fists continuing to fly. "Why..... why are you crying Ryan..... you shouldn't have done that to me." He stopped. "Oh God, I'm gonna kill you if you don't get out this house."

He watched as Ryan stood up slowly. "Hey wait. I'm going now."

"Then go," Preston yelled.

Ryan retreated. He wiped his eyes. When he approached the door he leaned on it, staring at Preston openly; his arm reached out to touch him. Preston shrank.

"Preston," he murmured, "what can I say? I'm a queer. I happen to love you. That isn't my fault..... just want you to know that..... you'll always be mine." He turned, slamming the door behind him. His footsteps could be heard for a few moments.

Preston gazed down at his mother's wedding picture stupefied. He looked down at his body and he remained there crying for a long, long while.

Sunday. It was raining beyond imagination. The apartment was quiet. Mrs. Wildey-King sat gazing at her broken wedding picture. Erica sat nearby indulging in her dime store novel. Preston was indolent on his bed, his heart heavy with remorse. Every now and again he would raise his head to sip his pepsi cola. He had drunk four cans and was comatose, but afraid to go to sleep. Ryan's face was indelible in his mind. Sometimes he opened his eyes in distress. He thought of Peggy. Do I still love her? Will I still feel something for her, or when I see a guy walking in front of me will I get...... excited?

Preston suddenly sat up. A mixture of fear, frustration and anger was within him. I have to see Peggy, he thought. Flinging on his shirt, a sinking sensation afflicted his stomach.

Walking along the beach Preston thought he would never be able to face Ryan again. The sun shone down warmly on his back, but it did not help to eliminate his depression. For two weeks he was forced to play hookey.

On arriving home one day, after roaming around on the beach, he opened the apartment door to hear his mother conversing anxiously with a familiar voice.

Recognising Mrs. Rosenberg's voice, he slid up to the closed door and listened intently with guilt spreading inside him.

"Well, I'm just worried; he hasn't been attending school for sometime now." There came a pause. "And his school work's failing as a result."

"I don't understand. He's been walking in and out of here for real. It beats me how he could be doing a thing like this."

"There's something else worrying me too. He seems, I don't know, withdrawn or very unhappy as he sits in class. The other kids tend to josh him occasionally......"

"Listen..... he seems perfectly happy at home. I mean, he has his ups and downs like any other adolescent."

"But don't you see, his school assignments are suffering due to his absence, Mrs. Wildey-King." She paused. "He has this good friend Ryan, they get along all right."

"You mean that dark chestnut haired boy, who always comes here?" Mrs. Wildey-King asked shortly. A cold chill ran down Preston's spine.

"Uh huh. He's a real nice boy. He laughs a lot, works pretty hard, but I'm not saying Preston doesn't. I mean, he used to, but not any more. He has something very dramatic on his mind; he looks that way nearly all the time."

"I don't know. Maybe it's to do with his friend Peggy. He has this......."

"Oh, he has a girlfriend? I don't mean to interfere with his personal life, everybody has a side of life they'd rather not discuss."

"But if this so-called personal life is affecting his school progress Mrs. Rosenberg, I think we have a right to discuss it."

There was a pause. Preston strained his ears, above the roars of the automobiles as they whizzed by the quiet apartment.

"Mrs. Wildey-King, I've been meaning to ask you something. You may not know yourself. Does your son drink or smoke pot? I mean, is he into alcohol?'

"What?"

"It is common, you know."

"Well no, I think. He is mad about pepsi cola, if that's what you mean."

"Pepsi cola?" Mrs. Rosenberg laughed suddenly. "Well, that seems to have enlightened me a little."

Preston's heart was palpitating. He pushed open the door, and walked into the lounge.

"Mrs. Rosenberg, you wanna talk to me?"

Mrs. Rosenberg rose, hand flying to horn-rimmed glasses. "Preston Wildey-King, where have you just sprung from?"

"Preston, where've you been?" his mother cried, also rising. "You haven't been to school, and I know that. So where've you been?"

"Preston, why weren't you at school today?"

Mrs. Rosenberg extended her hand to his shoulder. "Aren't you feeling too good?"

Preston shrugged his shoulders and smiled weakly. "Yeah. I feel different, that's all."

"Different?" yelled Mrs. Wildey-King, "What's so different huh?"

"Everything's different. I'm different. The whole world's different."

Mrs. Rosenberg frowned slowly. "Are you delirious, or high?"

"I'm neither," Preston replied. "You know, I feel terrific."

Mrs. Wildey-King came close to her son. "Preston, you know your school work's failing something awful when you act this way."

"Who said anybody's acting?" He glanced rapidly from his teacher to his mother.

"You know, you wouldn't be ditching school if your father was around."

Preston swallowed hard. "Well, he's not, is he?" He looked tranquilly at Mrs. Rosenberg's slender figure. In her blue cotton suit and her chignon hair style, she looked exactly like Nana Mouskouri; he wasn't into classical music anyway.

She caught his eye. "Um..... is there anything you'd like me to do for you?" Yeah, thought Preston wearily, undress and come to bed with me honey. "Like run you up to school in my beetle, I mean, it's not much of a car but we'll get there all right."

Preston laughed, waving his hand in the air. "Forget it."

"Preston, you just can't stay home all day, you know" said Mrs. Wildey-King sharply.

"I can too. Yeah, because I'm staying home anyways."

"What about your school work? Don't you care?" murmured Mrs. Rosenberg anxiously. "It'll suffer."

"You can hang that too."

Mrs. Wildey-King glanced at Mrs. Rosenberg, who nodded her head and hitched up her shoulder purse. "I guess Preston feels he doesn't need to come to school. We'll be having the vacation sooner or later."

"Yes Mrs. Rosenberg, I'll have a talk with him."

"You do that, Mrs. Wildey-King." She stared dismally at Preston for a moment. A dazzle of sunlight blinded her glasses. "Preston don't worry, we'll work things out okay. Just try to come out on Monday." She ambled past him, his mother walking ahead of her. Waving the car keys, Mrs. Rosenberg turned slowly.

"Preston, hey don't look so sad." She smiled. "You can come by my house sometime and I'll help you out with your maths. You know where I live, 3383 Roosevelt Drive. Okay? Come by anytime you like."

"Yeah, I'll think on that," Preston said absently. A stab of misery and excitement surged up in him.

His mother slammed the door. The apartment held its breath.

She glared at him, an austere expression on her oval face. "Preston, do you know what you're doing?"

He turned to go. "Yeah mom, I know what I'm doing."

She swung him around sharply. "No you do not know what you're doing. You are behaving like a childish kindergarten kid, who doesn't want to drink his milk."

Preston laughed. "Hey stop crying over spilt milk mom, you're acting as though I can't even think for myself yet." His eyes lit up with new anger as he stared at her sternly. "Well look at me mom, I'm 14 and a half years old, an 8th grade student, I know where I'm going, I know what I'm doing and I know what I want."

His mother's face changed. "What you want Preston, is a damn good beating, a shake up that I should have given you long ago. You're going to school come Monday whether you like it or not." She turned and walked down the short corridor, opening the kitchen door swiftly. "Yes you are," she yelled, "and don't tell me you're not."

At that moment the front door opened. Erica, with her book bag against her chest, stumbled in, her face lit up. "Hey, what's up with you Prezzie? Why you standing there like a cork screw about to go off, you all into having a party or something?"

Preston felt his muscles tighten. "Why'nt you just go to hell." He walked rapidly to his room and slammed the door shut.

He was looking at a poster attached to a stone wall, on the corner of the town's busiest street. Preston studied the coloured boy with huge white teeth, as he tilted a can of pepsi cola to his mouth; beside him was a bronze faced girl; she resembled Mrs. Rosenberg. His thoughts were interrupted by an emboldened "Hi". He whirled around. A sudden twinge of joy died away as he realised he was staring into the eyes of Lisa Kennedy.

"What're you doing by your lonesome?" A familiar, furtive smile passed her lips.

The sun was struggling to emit her last rays of heat, as a breeze threatened to dominate the sultry air.

"Walking," replied Preston.

"Oh you like walking, huh? Well now, how 'bout taking a walk someplace with me.... right?" Her eyes were brown. She had sharp features, unlike her sister, and a faint aroma of perfume lingered about her.

"Okay" Preston shrugged his shoulders. "If you like."

"Tell me," she almost purred as they walked along the wide crowded side walk, "what do you like doing best in life? And don't tell me it's nothing but sex."

Preston swept his eyes over the passing automobiles, the stores where tourists clustered by the hundreds, the emporium displaying junkie clothes, and the posters which seemed to animate the already enlivened street.

"I don't know. Drinking pepsi cola, I guess."

"Really?" She rubbed her shoulder to his, bumping it slightly. "Shall I tell you what I like doing?"

"I don't care."

"I like dating my sister's boyfriends, when she's not looking." She laughed abruptly. "And hey, it's fun, know what I mean?"

Preston felt his cheeks burn in confusion. "How should I know. I don't go around dating my sister's boyfriends do I?"

Lisa threw her hand on his shoulder. He felt a strange sensation pass through him, as she doubled over laughing. "Hey, you're so funny. You take things so seriously, but I think I'm beginning to like you, you know."

"Don't go any further," Preston laughed unsteadily. "If you do you better not tell Peggy."

"Okay" Lisa laughed again, throwing her other arm around his neck. They stopped walking. Preston found his eyes wavering nervously.

"I really hate my sister, don't you? She's all this and all that, you know."

"What does all this and all that mean?" Preston walked on, his eyes ahead of him. He felt Lisa's arm slide slowly down his back to his waist.

"Oh you know, all this'n that. Sometimes this sometimes that, I don't know."

"Well you ought to, she's your sister. I like her okay." Preston clamped his hand over her arm, as she tightened her grip around his waist.

"Well she likes you too..... in fact she loves you. I asked her why she was crying the other day, she told me she loves you too much. Isn't that crazy?"

A sudden squeeze around his heart made Preston slow down. His thoughts drifted back to that doleful day, when Peggy had made him cry. Now he was making her cry. He thought is this what love's all about, is that the only way to love somebody, by making each other cry?

Lisa leaned on him harder. "Hey, you really are the serious type aren't you? You don't even laugh."

Preston listened to her soft voice. "I laugh when I like, besides I'm stereotyped."

"Are you?" she sneered. "Then you don't really dig my sister do you?"

Preston looked at her challengingly. "Yes I do."

"Oh, and how come you haven't got her pregnant yet?" Her eyes narrowed. An intense heat ran through Preston. "What?"

"'C'mon you heard. Hey look Mr Stereotype's blushing." She pinched him gently, smiling sarcastically. "Yeah your face has really changed colour, you know. How come you make it go like that?"

Preston glanced up at the sky. "If I'm that red, then it must be the sun."

Lisa laughed and flung both her arms around his waist. They stopped. "You got fire in you, you know that boy..... huh?"

The world seemed to have come to a standstill. The streets had grown almost empty. A group of boys ambled past them inquisitively. They stopped half way, making weak wise cracks. "Hey sexy you turn me on," a long haired boy jeered, "and your friend there ain't that bad looking either." There was a chorus of laughter.

Preston turned around sharply, a surging anger rising inside him.

"Hey baby, I think they're jealous, don't you?" Lisa yelled monotonously.

"They could be."

"Then let's show them something they'll never forget." She flung herself closer into Preston's arms and kissed him on his lips. "Darling, I love you."

The air was filled with barbaric wolf whistles, as Preston tried to control the feelings arising in him.

"Whey, hey did you see that, guys?" A voice yelled, "did you see what she just done to that sucker?"

"Hey maybe we oughta go over there and teach the little lady how to do it the right way."

"Yeah maybe we ought to give her a few details."

Preston watched as they approached. A tall boy pushed him forcible off the sidewalk. "We don't want you, kid, we want this little chick here. We wanna give her a real big present."

Preston's eyes met Lisa's; they looked suddenly scared. The boy with the predatory expression on his face grabbed her by the shoulders.

"Get your hands off me, unless you want me to end your career," Lisa yelled.

The boy tried ineffectually to lift her up. She squirmed, kicked and lashed out as he fell back, shouting in pain.

"C'mon Preston, let's get out of here." And they ran, dodging across the street, avoiding automobiles as they went.

"Hey we know who you are," yelled the boy "we'll finish you off."

As they rounded the corner, Lisa stopped breathlessly, collapsing onto Preston's shoulder. "Hey – don't worry – I'm not – scared – of those dudes, okay?"

"You alright, huh?"

"Things like this always happen to me. I guess I'm just too vulnerable," she laughed. "What happens now?"

"Do I take you home?" Preston felt somewhat strange. "I mean, will you be safe on the street with them after you?"

"You're a real gentleman come to think of it, but no, I think Peggy'll go crazy if she sees me hanging in with you."

Preston gazed deeply into her eyes for a moment, he smiled cautiously. "I'll see you around sometime."

Lisa nodded her head, biting her lips thoughtfully. She plunked him on the shoulder gently. "Yeah, take care huh." She turned away. Preston watched her walk down the street. He eyed her pendulum hips and had a sudden desire to go after her.

When he arrived home, he combed his hair in the mirror. Studying his face carefully, he was conscious of his enticing features. They were more than attractive to himself; he thought they were attractive to everybody he came into contact with.

Lying on his bed, Preston tried hard to restrain himself from thinking of Lisa; he imagined her kissing him again. The room was quiet and airy, and a breeze drifted in through the open window. Preston's mind seemed out of control. For a moment he visualised Lisa's naked body; she touched him lightly over his bare chest; a tingling sensation ran right through his body down to his toes.

Preston opened his eyes. His hand drifted down to his waist, creating electric quivers as he urgently squeezed his genitals. He felt the stimulation simmer down; unzipping his jeans, he caressed them with both hands, as he listened to his palpitating heart. For a while he thought of Ryan; for a while he thought of Peggy. He rubbed harder as his paroxysm of excited emotion increased.

He slowly relaxed. He stared up at the ceiling, breathing harshly. It was a moment more superlative than he had ever experienced before.

Monday morning came. Preston sat miserably at the table as he eyed his mother calmly. Running her fingers through her thick hair, she stubbed out her cigarette, and stared at him sternly.

"Don't look at me like that, you're not ditching school today and that's flat."

Preston shielded the sun from his eyes. "I thought I'd call on Mrs. Rosenberg today, after school."

Erica looked up from her cereal. "Hoo-boy, is that your new girl friend Prezzie?"

"Why'nt you stick it?"

"For heaven's sake, you two, don't start now." Mrs. Wildey-King glanced at her watch. "It's fifteen of eight, you better make sure you call on your teacher Preston; she'll help you with your maths problem."

Ryan did not show for school. Preston thought about him, as he worked. He was somewhat relieved.

Mrs. Rosenberg did not look as though she was expecting Preston, when she opened the door of her suburban house that evening. Her eyes held a look of surprise and she smiled abruptly. "Hi there Preston." She paused; a gleam came to her brown eyes, "I'm glad you could come. Come on, come inside." Preston stepped cautiously into the sumptuous house.

His eyes swept over the expensive furniture, books, pictures, and occasional tables. Pictures illuminated the hallway; they dominated every door in every design. Pictures of liquid-eyed, solemn kids, people with large heads and stunted bodies, zig-zag pictures, leopard-skinned pictures, embroidery-stitched pictures, horizontal ancient pictures, naked women with lion's heads. Preston gazed stupefied; he thought it's like a historic art museum.

"You like the pictures?"

Preston turned. "Yeah, they're great." He nodded his head.

Mrs. Rosenberg smiled. "Preston we can study now, follow me." She led the way into a spacious, bright room. There were two green divans, but the room was dominated by a library of hard back volumes, paper backs and glossy magazines.

"Make yourself at home Preston." She sat down opposite on the divan. "Now where do we begin?"

Preston watched her perplexed expression, as she flicked through his books.

"What are your main problems?"

Preston shrugged. "Subtractions..... long divisions."

They worked silently, with Mrs. Rosenberg's brief demonstrations. Preston relaxed; he was enjoying her company and his work. The sun shone brightly through the large windows. Preston glanced around the room while she marked his exercises. He stared at a framed picture on a chest of drawers. Smiling, with a dark-haired man, was Mrs. Rosenberg on her wedding day; her brown hair cascaded down her shoulders, she looked much younger. A despondent feeling came over him; he tilted his head to her as she wrote swiftly over his work.

"Mrs. Rosenberg, I never realised you were married. I mean, I got so used to calling you Miss......."

She looked up impetuously, her face colouring slightly. "Yes Preston, I am." She stared at him for a while, then rubbed the ring on her finger and glanced at the photograph. "He's away in Europe actually, he's an architect." Preston glanced away. His eyes wandered around the room. "Did he design this house too?"

Mrs. Rosenberg laughed. "No, but this is the type of house he likes." She looked nervously at Preston, then averted her eyes around the room. "What do you make of it?"

Preston attempted a smile, and shrugged his shoulders. "It's something...... like out of my mom's magazine, you know."

A moment drifted by. Mrs. Rosenberg looked up. "Preston, would you like something to eat or drink? I mean, I have plenty of eats."

Preston looked up from his maths. His eyes met the large clock on the wall. It read half of seven. "No thanks, I never eat around this time." As the moments flitted by, Preston glanced up and diligently studied her occupied face.

When it was time to leave, he noticed her face did not hold her usual expression of concealment. It had a quiescent look about it. She lingered by the doorway. "I'll see you tomorrow evening, if that's okay."

"Okay." Preston descended the steps. The sun was setting behind a crimson sky. The air was tranquilly warm. All the houses in Roosevelt Drive were extravagant looking. Preston gazed at them, thinking of the apartment in which he lived.

Proceeding to cross at the intersection, Preston saw a tall black haired, hefty-looking boy walking his way. He glanced behind him; three more boys were swaggering toward him.

"Hey you, are you P.W. King?" The tall boy shouted.

Preston swallowed nervously and eased his hands out of his pockets.

"Hey, you deaf? I said do you go by the name of P.W. King?" The boy came closer, followed by the other boys, who were smoking cigarettes.

"Yeah. So what if I am?"

"So what? My name is Curt Miller, that's what." His grey eyes were angry in his square face. "I don't like guys taking girls from behind my back."

"You don't?"

"Yeah, and I won't let you put your hands all over my girl, hear?"

Preston felt a warm sweat breaking out under his armpits. "Yeah, and who's that?"

"Listen, don't get nifty with me."

"You wanna know something?" Preston took a step back. "Peggy Kennedy is through with you."

"The hell she is."

"She told me so."

"When?"

"Down by the beach."

"I don't believe you." A gleam passed his eyes. "Besides, she was lying in bed with me last night and she told me you're nothing but a low down creep. You wanna know something else?"

Preston shrugged his shoulders. He felt a twinge of anger.

"She's pregnant."

The impact of the words hit him sharply, playing over in his mind.

He looked closely at Curt Miller. "Who by?"

"Who by? The kid asks who by! You're looking at him right now."

"You're a smart assed liar."

"It'll hit you someday." He pushed him roughly.

Preston raised his fist, aiming a blow at his face. For a moment he stood there watching Curt Miller recoil slowly, his hands to his eyes. He backed away as Curt Miller suddenly looked up, water running from his eyes, and lunged forward. "What're you trying to do? Blind me?"

Preston felt a tightening pressure around his neck. He kicked out, fighting for air. Somebody seized his arms behind him as he felt an increasing pain in his stomach.

"Curt, you're gonna kill him."

"That's what I'm...... meaning to do."

Small distant voices entered Preston's ears. He opened his eyes wide as he saw the ground rush up to him. An army of footsteps seemed to be running away. "Leave him Curt, it's a cop."

A moment later Preston sat up. His eyes met the eyes of a coloured city policeman. "Say, are you alright kid?"

Preston slowly rose to his feet, helped by the large man. "I'm alright and I don't need any help." He eyed the six shooter on the man's hip for a moment, then he shook his dizzy head.

"Listen, I can give you a ride home." His voice carried a hint of sympathy. Preston looked at the black and white car; he was thinking if this cop hadn't come by he might have wound up dead. "No thanks, I'm okay." His voice shook. He turned and walked weakly up the street. I'm not gonna let them scare me, he thought.

Preston awoke to the sound of a ringing phone the next morning. His head was aching, his throat burned as he tried to swallow.

The door flew open; Erica in her nightgown flounced into the room. "Prezzie wake up, Peggy Kennedy's on the phone for you."

Preston jerked up suddenly. "How come you know it's her?" His voice croaked shakily.

"'Cause she told me so." She tossed her hair back, and ambled out.

Preston threw back his comforters, and gazed thoughtfully down at his feet. His heart palpitated strongly, as he approached the green phone. He picked the receiver up. "Hello – Preston speaking." He waited for her voice. A sharp sound came to his ears, a click, the phone went dead.

"Peggy?....." Preston slowly put the receiver in its cradle. He ambled to the refrigerator. Yanking out a pepsi cola, he thought seriously of Peggy, he thought of Curt Miller, his heart raced.

Preston watched her step out of the drug store; for a moment he ambled cautiously behind her. It was Wednesday evening, the air whispered breezily through his hair. "Hey, Peggy."

She stopped abruptly and turned around; her face crimsoned slightly as she stared at him.

Preston swallowed hard. "Hey Peggy, why'd you phone me the other day?"

She dropped her eyes, turning away. "I don't wanna talk, okay?"

He walked rapidly beside her. "You do wanna talk. Isn't that why you phoned?"

Her blue eyes lifted suddenly. "There is nothing to talk about – "

"You phoned me Peggy. Sure..... then you hung up..... why?"

She stopped, running her hand through her hair. "I'm going crazy thinking about us two, you know."

Preston eyed her suspiciously. "You mean Curt Miller don't you. He told me a few things –"

"Yeah, he jumped you."

"You set him up to that?"

She walked on. "Ask me no questions and I'll tell you no lies."

Preston restrained himself from grabbing her. "Yeah, well let me tell you something. I – I know you're pregnant."

"What?" she hissed, whirling around. A few passers-by turned also. "Preston, where in god's name did you get that roorback from?"

Preston stared at her uneasily. "The guy who jumped me and –"

"Listen, I am through with Curt Miller, so just shuddup about it."

"You sent him to tell me that you're pregnant, right? So that I'd just forget about you, right?"

She glanced up. "Listen, you can believe whatever you

want to, but I'm through with Curt, and he did not make me pregnant."

A compact automobile screeched round the corner. The air suddenly breathed in, causing the sun to beat down more powerfully. Preston looked at the brown grocery bag in Peggy's arms. "What'd you buy back there?"

"Hey, what is this, twenty questions?"

"Peggy," he lowered his eyes, "I think it's time we should get back together."

There was a long pause. She stopped and leaned against a tree. The shouts of children playing in the verdant park seemed to drop to a lower note. "I think we already have, don't you?" Her eyes met his.

Preston felt a hot sensation, his heart raced. "If we make up, Peggy, how am I to know that you won't run off with some other – "

"I love you." A softness came into her eyes. "Will you believe that for a while?"

His stomach jumping, Preston abruptly heard his heart pounding in his ears. He stared at her intensely. "I haven't stopped loving you since the first day we met, you know that."

A faint, distinguished smile awoke over her lips, her eyes looked away. Preston ran on quickly. "I didn't look at the other cheerleaders. I always looked at you, even when I was playing."

She glanced back. "No wonder your team was always losing, you weren't paying attention."

Preston laughed. "I wanted to impress you, I guess."

For a moment their eyes transfixed, then she dropped her stare seriously.

"Listen, Preston I haven't been myself lately, I need time to think it over."

Preston nodded his head emphatically.

"I have a lot of studying to do," she raised her eyes, "so don't get me wrong if we don't see each other for a while, okay?"

"Okay." There was an awkward silence. Preston felt a provocative sensation well up inside him; he moved closer to her.

She flinched and turned away. "Don't Preston.. please....."

"Why not? What's the matter with you, huh?"

"Nothing. I have to get home, okay?" She started to walk away. "I'll phone you sometime."

"Whenever you like." Preston watched her among the crowded park, until her pink blouse disappeared, in a rainbow of assorted colours. He thought weakly; she really doesn't understand me at all.

He was sitting crosslegged on his bed, one fine evening, listening to Buddy Holly's hit record Peggy Sue, when the door bell rang. He jerked and put the pepsi cola he was drinking on the dresser.

Erica was out at a disco, his mother was attending her weekly Jehovah Witness Session. He made his way to the door.

"What do you want?" he said to Ryan, who was standing placidly, his face slightly cut. "I just wanna talk, okay?"

Preston pushed the door forcibly. "Go to hell." He felt the pressure of Ryan's foot against the door.

"Hey Preston." His eyes resembled an affectionate cocker spaniel's, his face seemed somewhat mature. "Let's – let's make nice huh. I didn't mean to harm you that other day."

Fright together with anger took hold of him; Preston slammed the door shut in his face.

The next day at Mrs. Rosenberg's house he found his mind straying absently to Ryan's face. Frustrated, he put his pen down and glanced at the dark haired woman.

"What's the problem now Preston? You still can't figure out that sum? We're gonna be here a long while," she laughed.

"I don't think I feel like working right now." He lay back on the divan, spreading his arm on the back and gazed at her impertinently.

Mrs. Rosenberg took off her glasses, rubbing her forehead. "I feel exhausted too. Maybe we're overworking ourselves."

"Maybe." Preston inspected her without her glasses. She looked different. His stomach churned, confused.

"You like a drink to ease your mind a little?"

"What kind of drink?"

She waved her hand to the mahogany cabinet holding glasses, many bottles of whiskey, soda water and bourbon. "Anything you want, like my home made wine."

Preston immediately felt thirsty. "Anything I want?"

She nodded her head, putting back on her glasses. "That is unless you'd prefer some milk or coffee."

"No thanks. I'll have some of that wine please." He watched as she ambled over to the cabinet and unscrewed a large bottle. Feeling a strange excitement Preston let the sweat creep down his back.

She returned, carrying two neat glasses and handed one down to him as she sipped hers slowly. "My husband and I often indulge in this kind of thing, when we both feel tuckered out."

Preston could only perceive the acid needle in his throat as he swallowed the wine.

"It's not a conventional thing, if you know what I mean."

He glanced up; his mind felt tranquilized. "I don't drink much you know."

Mrs. Rosenberg turned around to sit opposite him. "You're all for pepsi cola I guess," she nodded her head approvingly. "Yes, that's really good. In fact, I shouldn't really be giving you this."

Preston knocked back his head.

"Hey, don't drink so fast!" she extended her arm slightly, laughing. "It's a little strong."

"I hit off with this kind of thing okay. It's already making me feel easy."

"That's what it's supposed to do."

Preston glanced at his empty glass. It's making me drunk, he thought. An aching pain struck his shoulders.

"You don't really want any more do you?"

Preston closed his eyes sharply and he felt like going to sleep. "No thanks Mrs. Rosenberg..... I gotta....... get home."

"So soon? But I guess you feel tired. So do I." She rose, taking Preston's glass.

He watched with lassitude as she placed it on the coffee table. The room seemed to be staring at him. He got up. "I'll..... see you tomorrow Mrs....... Mrs. Rosenberg, and thanks for the drink."

"You're welcome Preston, and be on time for school tomorrow, okay?"

He felt her hand on his back as he went out the door. "You forgot your jacket."

"Thanks Mrs. Rosenberg." The fresh air opened his eyes. "So long."

Opening the door to the apartment, Preston smelled a familiar aroma of cigarette smoke. He closed the door softly behind him and hung his jacket up. Turning his eyes to the lounge, he heard a laugh, coming from a nearby room. Curiously he trod softly to Erica's closed bedroom door.

A groan, followed by a frivolous laugh, reached Preston's ears. He listened attentively, putting his hand furtively to the door handle.

"Can you imagine the way I feel about you?" Erica whispered.

"Shush babe, let's go easy on this," replied the ardent, male voice.

"Hey, not so rough." An infectious murmur escaped the room.

"Oh..... I'm gonna have a...... million marks on.... my back after this honey....." A loud sigh "go on go on....."

"Erica...."

Preston flung open the door. His mind reeled with what he saw. Erica was laying naked, except for a white sheet, on the bed. Beside her lay a muscular looking boy. He sat up, grabbing at the sheets. "Hey, who's that?"

She looked up, a look of surprise dominating her angular face. "That's my brother. What're you standing there for Bobby, get up."

"Maybe he wants to join us," the boy laughed.

Preston gazed at his sister; she made no attempt to cover herself.

"Looks like he ain't never seen a girl before."

"Hey, is mom back or something?" Erica asked.

Preston eyed the boy. "No." He turned, closing the door. Stupid with sleepiness he headed to his room.

Sometime during the night, he awoke to a loud shuffling noise. He sat up, his tee shirt clinging to him damply.

"Preston?" A voice whispered.

"Yeah?" He visualised Erica's face in the dark.

"You won't tell mom what you saw back there will you?"

Preston closed his eyes; he lay back. "No I won't tell, but who was the guy?"

"Just a guy." She sat on the edge of the bed. "It's not the first time I lay with him, you know."

Preston gazed at the ceiling. "How many times have you done it in this here house?"

There was a pause. "Oh, just this once. Are you gonna let on to mom?"

"I don't know. I guess not."

They sat in silence for a while, listening to the sounds of night. The whirr of the refrigerator, the ticking of a clock, which read half of two, and the sounds of one another's breathing.

"Will you Preston? I'll be glad if you don't. I admit I've been bad to you. But that's over now, huh?"

Preston took a deep breath. "I guess so." He closed his eyes, too weak to take his tee shirt off. When he opened them Erica had gone, and the darkness was fading to an overall light. He made his way to the kitchen. Opening the refrigerator, he took one of the five remaining cans of pepsi cola and drank.

In school, Mrs. Rosenberg was looking her usual self. Ryan sat placidly in the front row; occasionally he turned and glanced at Preston spontaneously.

The sun was hot on Preston's face; he began to think he would pass out if he did that all day. He was relieved to be outside when school ended. The shouts and laughs of students around the campus were harsh to Preston's ears. He tried ineffectually to see Peggy in the crowds. It was while he was ambling along the parched sidewalk, that he heard a voice call his name. He immediately swung around, and spotted Ryan's lean figure running across the street toward him.

"Hey Preston," he yelled, "wait, I wanna talk with you."

Preston felt the blood rush to his cheeks; he turned, walking more vigorously.

"Hey Preston, hang on there." Ryan's footsteps were audible. Preston felt an arm around his shoulder. He went suddenly cold.

"Hey you don't have to give me the pass up, we can still be friends."

Preston pushed his arm off his shoulder; he stared at him critically. "Hey Ryan, do me a favour will you, get outta my life." He looked away, embarrassed. "I don't wanna be in the same house as you, the same room, I don't wanna know you anymore."

Ryan raised his hand. "Hey man, you don't really mean that?"

Preston flinched as he touched his cheek. "We've been friends too long to break up now." A deafening roar of an automobile passed by.

Preston willed his eyes to look at him. "Get outta the way Ryan. I don't like fairies." He tried to move, as Ryan threw an arm around his waist.

"Hey babe, I'm only human –"

"Get off, Ryan." Preston clenched his jaws. He swung round, grabbing him by his shirt. "Don't you ever so much as touch me again."

Ryan suddenly toppled backwards, as he let go of him. It was like a slow motion picture. Preston watched as he bounced onto the street, mixing with zooming automobiles. He turned away sharply. A screech of brakes, a girl screaming. Preston looked back. Ryan was rising to his feet shakily, his face white, a curious look in his eyes. For a moment they stood there, staring at each other.

The woman from the brown Mustang, her mouth open, ran up beside Ryan, touching him gently, smoothing his hair. People gathered round tightly, their eyes drifting toward Preston. He turned away, his heart pounding, his throat stinging. He thought, do I hate him so much, so that I wanna kill him? Preston glanced down at his shaking hands. He looked back at Ryan and quickened his pace.

What are friends for? Preston asked himself seriously as he walked to Mrs. Rosenberg's house. They hate you. They love you. They destroy you. They're there to comfort you, when you need them. They're like your own brothers and sisters.

"Hi Preston, come on in." Mrs. Rosenberg was standing there, smiling. She gestured behind her. "I marked your work this morning and it seems very good, you know." She led the way into the study. "There are a few small mistakes, but I'm sure you'll find them easy once you work them out."

Preston took his seat on the divan. He remembered the sharp taste of the home made wine, with pleasure. Glancing at Mrs. Rosenberg he saw her face was corrugated with thought.

"You know, the wine we had last night," he swallowed, "It really made me sleep good."

She looked up from the books briefly. "It did? I don't suppose it made you work any better?"

Preston laughed. "How many did I do wrong?"

"Ten or eleven." She raised her eyebrows, handing him his blue maths book, and pointed down to the corrections outlined in red ink.

He took a pen from his jacket, proceeding to write down the requested answers. He felt Mrs. Rosenberg's eyes on him for a while, then she rose silently, walked through the open door and closed it firmly behind her. Although the room was shaded from the sun, Preston began to feel sleepy. He took off his jacket absently, as his mind worked out the sums. Every part of the room fell asleep.

It awoke when Mrs. Rosenberg stepped back in the room. Preston glanced up. She was clad in jeans, a white almost transparent tee shirt, and her hair hung loose about her shoulders. She looked refreshed as she sat down opposite. Preston found it extremely hard to avert his eyes from her. He went hot.

"You like reading, Preston?" she asked after a while.

Preston's head was spinning. He put his pen in his mouth, biting on it hard. "I don't get to read so much."

"Only.... I notice that your English is getting really impressive now." Her hands gesticulated. "You have an intelligent way of putting your words, almost as though you enjoy writing in a special way."

Preston smiled. "I don't know 'bout that. I just do what's expected of me." His eyes slipped down to her cloche-shaped breasts. He was aware of a concupiscence running through his mind.

"What exactly do you like doing, Preston?"

He trembled slightly, "Do – do you mean my school subjects, or – or my main interests outside school?"

Mrs. Rosenberg put one side of her sleek hair behind her ear. "Oh, anything you specifically like doing." She removed her glasses from her sharp-featured face; they hung momentarily in the air.

Anybody can guess what a teenage guy like me is interested in, Preston thought. "I like listening to music, taking walks on the beach, and –"

"I too like listening to music Preston. I'm not into hot or anything, I prefer classical."

Preston eyed the framed picture of Mr. Rosenberg. He was thinking he looked like his own father, taut face, wide shoulders. "What are your other interests?"

Mrs. Rosenberg replied emphatically, "I love art. I think it's a terrific skill to draw such lovely forms of life." She stared down at her wedding ring, twisting it. "..... I also enjoy making..... wine."

There was a brief constrained silence. Preston bit his lip. "You like doing maths?"

She laughed provocatively, the air broke up. "Do I like doing maths?" Her hand flew to her breasts. Preston eyed them cautiously.

"To be honest with you Preston, no I detest them. It's a real big headache." She laughed again, tossing her hair back strenuously.

Preston put his pen down. "Why'd you become a teacher?"

Her smile slowly faded. "Why did you ask me that?"

Preston shrugged. He breathed deeply, as his body went hot, then cold. For a moment he was conscious of where he was. In his teacher's house, talking to a woman he did not know, who confused him until he felt strange sensations whenever he thought of her.

He studied her carefully. "You look real nice without your glasses Mrs. Rosenberg."

She crimsoned, sensitively. "Don't call me Mrs. Rosenberg, it sounds so formal. Call me Connie."

"Connie?.... that's an attractive name." Preston's knees went suddenly weak.

"Oh, you think so?.... my husband sometimes calls me Constance."

Their eyes met. Her face brightened.

"Preston, tell me, how do you manage to have such extraordinary eyes?"

Preston's heart leapt. "I don't pay much attention to my eyes Mrs. Rosenberg. Connie." He laughed, confused.

"Doesn't it run in the family, or are you just one of the lucky people?"

"I don't know what you mean –"

"Come on, you can do better than that, you –"

"Alright, alright, supposing I told you my dad had eyes like mine."

She smiled, rolling her eyes. "I'd believe you." Her expression changed. She gazed at him, as though studying an interesting painting. A smile played around her face. "You're a very attractive boy Preston, you have the most sincere looks; did anybody ever tell you that, huh?"

Preston refused to be flattered. He shrugged his shoulders. "Hey, I noticed how good looking you are too, Connie."

"Don't fawn on me Preston." She raised her eyebrows. "Besides my husband wouldn't like it if he knew I was making nice with one of my own 8th grade students."

"Then why'd you invite me here?"

"Because...." She closed her eyes quickly. "I thought it might do you some good, and..... I guess I need the company."

Preston nodded his head, as the sweat poured down his back. "I need company too you know."

She raised her eyes. "Then that makes two of us." She laughed.

Preston anxiously waited for the next evening to arrive. Mrs. Rosenberg cheerfully yelled to him to come right in, she was in the lounge. Preston eyed her curiously, as he stepped in. She was sitting on the divan, clad in a sky-blue dress, which reached her ankles. Her feet were bare, her toe nails painted bright red; on her face she wore the expression of the Mona Lisa.

"Hi Mrs. Rosenberg."

She smiled, tilting her head. "I asked you to call me Connie."

Preston sat down opposite her. "You want me to call you that at school too?"

"If you must." She smirked. "But seriously, when you refer to me as Mrs. Rosenberg..... it makes me feel twice your age."

Preston looked at her closer. "Well aren't you?"

"I am no liar when it comes to age." Her eyes drifted away. "When I was a pimpled face fifteen year old teenager, you were just making your first, wobbly steps into life."

Preston laughed. "Not true. I started walking at six months, rode my first two wheeler at three, bought my own records at six, and started to take an interest in girls when I was eight."

"Wow, that's something, you'll be telling me that you're married next."

Preston gazed at her. "That, I think, is something that I can control."

Mrs. Rosenberg reached over to the table for her glasses. "Come with me Preston, I want to show you something."

Preston rose, following her down the hall into a spacious, breezy room. She extended her arm to a brightly coloured painting of a large eyed, innocent boy, with a mop of curly hair.

"What do you make of that?"

Preston stared at the boy's face. A cold tremble ran through him. The boy's eyes seemed to be pleading for something. It reminded him of Ryan. He swallowed hard. "It's nice – sad but nice."

"I like sad drawings. I painted it myself."

"It's great. Who's the guy?"

She turned to look at him. "A guy I once knew, back in Santa Barbara. He's a big man now, with a family of his own."

The breeze and the door were having a disturbing fight, in which the door lost. It slammed shut, sending sensations of loneliness through Preston's mind.

He glanced at Mrs. Rosenberg warily. "Did you ever think of having kids Connie?"

A shadow passed her face. "I have plenty of time for kids. Besides, Leif and I, thought it wouldn't be fair, with him going to Europe all the time."

Preston shifted the hair from his eyes.

"C'mon, let's go back in the lounge, huh?" She turned suddenly. "We won't do maths. We'll just talk. I'll fix you a drink, a schooner, you like that?"

"Okay." Preston thought, this is probably the way she'd treat her kids, too.

Mrs. Wildey-King glanced up from the newspaper. "How's your maths coming along Preston?"

Preston kept his eyes fixed on the television. A warmness spread over his face. "It's getting better."

"I'm glad to hear that." The newspaper rustled. "I hope your visits to Mrs. Rosenberg are worth while."

"They are." Preston rose quickly. The phone rang three times; he was thinking, it has to be Peggy.

"It's for you mom."

Mrs. Rosenberg opened the door. Her eyes were gleaming as she beckoned him inside. Preston, taking off his jacket, noticed her cream, bare-backed dress with interest. He followed her into the lounge. She sat down on the divan a moment later, and handed him a drink.

"It's Pina Colada, you'll like it."

Preston felt her flagrant eyes on him. As he took a sip of the drink, he glanced up. The sun was beginning to set, the air remained excessively hot.

"Jesus, I hate the summer. It's so hot."

Preston shrugged his shoulders. "I guess it wouldn't be summer, if it weren't hot."

"And it would definitely not be winter, without nice warm fires and mugs of steaming hot chocolate." Mrs. Rosenberg laughed.

"You like winter time, huh?"

She rapidly swallowed her drink. "Winter is me. I love it. I mean, what would I do without it?..... The cold frostly air as I wake up in the mornings.... the feeling that you just gotta be warm."

"You're not really that anti-summer are you?"

She nodded her head emphatically, rotating her glass in her hands.

"Do you like the drink?"

Preston glanced at his glass. "Uh-huh. It's terrific. What's it made of?"

"What's it made of?" She gesticulated her free arm in the air. "Rum, little coconut oil, pineapple juice. I mean, it's sweet and it could be pretty strong."

There was a short silence; cicadas croaked outside. Preston's mind swayed as he gazed at Mrs. Rosenberg.

"Say, how about some music." She stood up unsteadily. "I have millions of Beethoven overtures. I mean, it'd most probably take you all year to plough through them."

Preston raised his eyebrows, as she turned to the mahogany stereogram.

"I really love Tchaikovsky's Swan-Lake, it makes my heart quiver."

"I prefer pop music."

She whirled around. "Preston, can you dance? Yeah, maybe I should put some easy music on, then you can dance with me."

Preston eyed her timidly. "I'm not much good at dancing."

"Sure you are." For a while the room was silent, as she flicked through the piled-high albums. Preston drained his glass.

"Listen, how about this one." She waved the record. "It's the Commodores', 'Three Times a Lady'." Putting the music on, she swayed her body, starting to dance herself toward Preston. He took her hand as she pulled him up; he felt the sweat tingling his nose as he got closer to her.

"That's..... my..... baby.... you..... just..... rest your head on my..... shoulder...... relax...." Preston could feel the tension ebbing away from him; he leaned on her, a sweet scent invading his nostrils. He felt her hands slide up his back, over his chest; she murmured the words to the song – "There's... nothing..... to.... keep us.... apart." For a long while they swayed to the music, each note making the room echo, each sentence crying out passionately. Preston was thinking, it could go on for ever.

The music faded away. Preston found it difficult to let go, they clung to each other for a while. Mrs. Rosenberg pulled away gently. Preston flopped down on the divan and watched her body with excitement as she bent over to change the record. All the embarrassment slipped away, as a powerful sensation invaded his body. Preston glanced down at his legs; he opened them wider; a quiver circulated between them.

"This is another slow number." Mrs. Rosenberg's voice had changed. She turned around, her eyes like blue marble. "I like Rose-Royce records, especially this one."

The music penetrated Preston's thoughts. "What's this called?"

She smiled, walking toward him and knelt down beside the divan. "I'm Wishing on a Star." She gazed up dreamily, her hand on his thigh, caressing it with rhythm. Preston closed his eyes, enjoying her touch. He felt his tee shirt clinging hotly to his back. His eyes flew open. Mrs. Rosenberg was tugging, pinching his chest.

"Take it off.... take off this thing." She pushed his tee shirt up to his shoulders. Preston felt coolness as his chest was exposed. He felt her hands slowly travel down to the belt of his levis; she unbuckled it, glancing up furtively. Preston's heart palpitated. His levis were down to his knees, leaving him in his white under-pants. He watched with growing arousement as she caressed his legs, sliding her hand up, getting faster as the music changed tempo.

For a moment Preston let her touch his genitals, then as her hand went under the elastic, he clamped his hand firmly over hers. She looked up, her face tender. Taking his hand she placed it on her breasts and leaned forward. Preston came down, his lips parted, his passion increasing, as he kissed her. He squeezed her breast, sweeping his mouth over her cheeks, down to her neck, biting into her; she gasped.

A moment passed, they separated, staring into each other's eyes. "Preston I love this," she whispered hoarsely. "but let's go some place nice." The music was still playing; a curtain had fallen over the room.

She rose slowly, grasping his hand. Preston let her pull his levis off completely, throwing them across the room. She pulled him up and together they ambled through the room. Preston stopped at the doorway and glanced back briefly, his eyes falling on Leif Rosenberg. A feeling of guilt swept over him.

He felt a warm arm slide around his bare waist; he turned; she was smiling anxiously. He followed her up a winding staircase, through to a white-painted room with an extravagant brass-railed bed. Mrs. Rosenberg let go of him and ambled to the bed. Sweeping the comforters back, she began to un-zip her dress.

Preston lingered by the door. He found he was throbbing internally, a frustrated passion boiled inside him.

"C'mon Preston babe..." She stepped out her dress. Her body was slim, her breasts high; she moved forward erotically.

Preston's passion intensified. Everything seemed unrealistic as he embraced her, he felt her hands drag down his under-pants.

Together they fell on to the bed. Preston pressed hard ardently against her, kissing her violently over and over again.

Mrs. Rosenberg's eyes enlarged; she breathed deeply, as their bodies joined with rhythm. Her face broke out in sweat, her nostrils flared, she uttered Preston's name between each kiss, from suddenly swollen lips.

This was more than all the sex movies Preston had ever seen. A sharp pang ran through him; the happiness he had craved for met him with bewilderment. He gasped for air as he drew away. He lay back panting. He stared at the ceiling.

"You're so sensual so mature." She caressed his chest. "You're the best – you're the king."

Preston closed his eyes tight for some time. Unaccountably he found himself feeling depressed. He had committed himself to this woman, he did not know why. He was no longer a virgin. He ached with the most powerful sensuality.

A moment passed. "Connie." She leaned over, her breath hot. "I don't know who I am anymore."

"No," she whispered earnestly. "You're something, you're a smart, sensitive, beautiful boy. Preston I am in love with you."

"Yeah." He tried to smile; he had a mixture of pain, exhaustion and confusion rising up inside him.

"What're you gonna be when you grow up?" Preston did not respond. "You're gonna be a lady-killer, you know, you're only a kid and I can't keep my hands off you."

"I can't keep my eyes off you." Preston leaned over, he kissed her, he stroked her wet hair, sighing.

"What is it, sweet boy?"

Preston's eyes were blurry, the tears of emotion burned them intensely. He lay back on the pillow. For some reason thoughts of Peggy, then Ryan, came crashing back to him.

"Hey.... take it easy honey." Mrs. Rosenberg's face changed. "It's not the end of the world."

The next few days Preston's appetite for pepsi cola increased. For some time he forgot that food existed; drinking the fizzy liquid seemed to console him as the heat of the day intensified.

Lying on his bed, his hands tucked between his legs, he thought of Mrs. Rosenberg's smiling face. He re-lived each moment in his mind with a wild paroxysm of desire. Fire ran right through his body. His thoughts drifted on to Ryan, he rolled over. He dreamed of Peggy; he woke up in a sweat.

One night, he woke with a sensation of drowning. A wet blanket of cold sweat enveloped his body. A soft pressure lay against his forehead, and he focused his eyes into the ebony darkness. A shadow hovered over him. Preston's mouth dropped open as he jerked up.

"Alright, alright, shush now." His mother's voice was a whisper. "You screamed out."

For a moment Preston thought it was Mrs. Rosenberg. Over-come with sleepiness, he lay back down.

"What's the matter, baby?"

He tried to talk. Tempestuous thoughts dominated his mind. He felt fingers running over his eyes.

"Hey, don't cry like that. What's the matter, huh? All you do is drink and sleep, tell me what's troubling you."

"I'm not crying mom."

A quietness circled the room. "It's only a passing phase..... you'll get over it." She stroked his damp hair, she blew on him gently. "You're beginning to act just like you did when your father died."

Sitting on the beach one day, with the air feeling cool on his face, Preston glanced up to see Ryan ambling along toward him. A frustrated, depressed mood was in him; he had no desire to move when Ryan sat down beside him. He remained immobile gazing out at the cerulean sea.

"Hey, long time, no see," Ryan said, with forced cheerfulness.

There was an elaborate silence. The shouts of people playing frisbee on the cool sand reached Preston's ears. The flap of the rapid waves gave him a solitary feeling.

"Do you remember when we first met?" Ryan's composed voice brought Preston back to reality. "I can remember, we were sitting right here, on July 4th, listening to the waves and drinking coley. Everybody was having clam-bakes. My brothers picked you up and dragged you into the water." Preston bit his lip. "Boy, were you screaming, you were laughing too. Everybody was laughing... on the way home, we all sang songs, and Aaron nearly got knocked over, by a beetle, but I think that was one of the happiest days I ever had... those don't come by too often."

"It was always like July 4th in those days," Preston said slowly, "but now..... and to think that I've known you so long Ryan, I can't believe that you're a fairy." He glanced at Ryan. His head was hanging down between his knees. He looked fragile and diminished.

"Believing is for-free," Ryan said. "So why can't we make-believe that we're friends again?"

Preston considered his words. They ran rapidly through his mind; he remembered the dreadful day he had almost killed his best friend.

"Ryan." He swallowed urgently. "We are friends, okay? Don't give me a hard time, we'll be friends until the day we die."

"But'll never be the same as before." His voice shook. "You'll never trust me again." They stared at each other, for the first time. Preston, feeling embarrassed, glanced away.

The sea-gulls were circling in the sky, shrieking out notes of pity. The air was as still as death.

Preston glanced back at Ryan; his shoulders were heaving, he was crying. A guilty feeling roused inside him. He put his arm cautiously around Ryan's shoulders. "Hey Ryan, don't do this to me. I hate to see you this way." He stared at the tears as they fell, each one like a glistening diamond. "Maybe we should both try to forget what happened back there..... but it's gonna be hard."

The sun was visibly going down as Preston and Peggy made their way into St. Louis' cafeteria. A sultry aroma of potato, French fries, filled the room. Customers in bright coloured clothes, took their ease on red divans situated behind wooden tables, which were laid out with drinks and exotic dishes of food. Their attention was on to a colour television, resting at the rear of the bar. Preston glanced awkwardly behind him, in front of him, around him. A boy with an earring in his ear was holding hands across the table with a girl, in a corner. A tall, blonde haired girl was standing patiently by the bar; she glanced at Preston, then averted her heavily made-up eyes to Peggy.

Preston turned his attention to the television. He sat opposite Peggy on the soft foamed divan.

"What'll we have?" she whispered "you want something to eat, huh?"

Preston shrugged his shoulders. "I don't think so."

"How about a big Mac hamburger?.... you don't have to eat it now."

Preston abruptly shook his head.

"You can take it home in a doggie-bag."

"I'm not hungry, okay."

Peggy rose, her smile threatening to fade. "I'll buy you one anyway."

"I won't eat it; hey, you can buy me a pepsi-cola."

There were a few hushes from behind him. Preston glanced around timidly. His eyes rested on two brunette girls, who gazed back at him with equal curiosity. The girl with the full lips smiled provocatively, her hands wrapped around a 7 up. The other girl winked her eye. Preston turned away, feeling suddenly hot, in his white tee shirt. The sun was a fire, slowly dying down on the wooden tables. A commercial, with Joe Frazier commenting about a brand of beer, surrounded by a chorus of coloured singers, flitted past the screen. Preston eyed Peggy as she came strolling back, clad in tight jeans and a blue Dacron blouse.

She plonked the hamburgers and two large tumblers down on the table; she tossed her hair back, sitting down. "There you go."

Preston reluctantly took his hamburger, dripping with Worcester sauce, and sipped the drink. He felt an irritation, as his lips brushed the polythene tumbler, followed by an acid pang on his tongue. "Hey, what is this stuff?"

Peggy tilted her head as she nibbled at the hamburger. "Coca-cola."

"Listen, I don't like that. I like Pepsi-cola."

"Pepsi-cola, Coca-cola, what's the difference?" Her tone was suddenly sarcastic.

"A hell of a lot of difference, you know that?"

The fat man leaning on the bar, his mouth full of potato chips, whirled around. Three heavily made-up girls, their eyebrows knitted, turned around. A long blond haired man whirled around, his eyes piercingly blue, a cigarette dangling from his mouth. A middle-aged couple, a scrawny youth, an elderly man, they all turned their attention directly to Preston.

Preston lowered his eyes angrily. He felt the hair on the nape of his neck rise stiffly, the sweat breaking out under his armpits, hot and cold at the thought of so many eyes on him. Peggy let her hamburger hang momentarily in the air, her face became a mask of hatred mixed with embarrassment.

"Hey, what's with you guys back there, can't you shuddup?" The corpulent paternal man by the bar slapped a white cloth over his shoulder. He ambled noisily over to Preston, his jaws working as he fought to swallow the excessive chips in his mouth.

"We are trying to watch this goddam movie." His eyes bulged, his cheeks welled up like balloons; red veins streaked his face. "What in God's name is the matter with you son?"

A question that had repeated itself from the day he was born. Preston saw a vision of his father, working away at a mangled bicycle. The day he had gone crazy, riding it down a steep street and colliding with a parked automobile, was the day a part of him died away.

He looked up uncertainly. "Who said anything was the matter?" His eyes met Peggy's. She screwed up scornfully.

"Then shuddup, okay, shuddup and watch the movie, huh." The man turned away, then glanced back. "Or get up and get out, I won't care."

A short silence, then one by one each head turned away, fixing disturbed attentions back to the television.

Preston watched anxiously as Peggy placed her hamburger down, her mouth set. She leaned across the table. "Are you having some kind of permanent erection?" she whispered. "Why'd you get all worked up over a lousy drink of pepsi-cola, huh?..... you know, sometimes Preston, you're just a lousy pain in the ass..... I want you to know that, okay?"

Preston, feeling more hurt than angry, nodded his head fixedly. He put down his hamburger, pushing the tumbler away from him. For a moment he watched Peggy's profile as she ate and watched television. The room began to slowly close up, and a pressure of suffocation increased. A moment later Preston experienced a cold sensation, people's heads were swimming around him, the colours flashed by his eyes in an orgy of kaleidoscopic patterns. He felt his head meet the table; a wave of nausea, then everything was quiet, cosy warm and dark.

When Preston awoke, he felt an aching throbbing pain in his neck. He glanced around stiffly. Every table was vacant, the whole of the cafeteria was empty except the bartender, who was piling odd chairs on to tables and sweeping the floor near the red juke box. An apprehensive thought struck Preston; he looked frantically around for Peggy. The windows were less steamed up, the inky darkness outside looked like an open mouth.

"Hey mister," he croaked. His head became suddenly clear, on hearing his voice. The man whirled around. "Oh, so you're awake now, are you. Listen, next time you wanna sleep, go home to your cot, okay?" He put down the broom, striding over to Preston. "Time's up, get going now. Unless you wanna help me wash-up?"

Preston strained his neck. "Wait a moment..... what happened to the blonde girl who was sitting right here?"

"She left about three hours ago if you must know, and that ain't my business, okay." He clamped a hand on Preston's wrist. "C'mon, your folks'll be getting worried 'bout you, so move it now."

Preston got up feebly, noticing that the television was off. His throat was dry. As he stepped out the cafeteria, the warm night air sent strange shivers down his back. He walked slowly around the corner, his body slouched, his shadow following on the sidewalk, under the light of the moon. Preston's thoughts were jumbled up over Peggy; his heart pounded as he visualised again her strong, angry face. Why was everybody always getting mad at him?

Footsteps attracted his attention. He glanced up. Through the beam of a street light he spotted four swaggering figures headed his way. He stopped, hands out of his pockets, as the smallest figure started to run toward him. It was the way he ran, the way he waved his arms, Preston realised it was Ryan.

"Hey, Preston, where've you been, huh?" He slapped an arm round him tightly, as his brothers came up toward him.

"We've been looking for you," Ashley chided.

Ryan put his face close to his. "We're gonna hit off that store now Preston, remember?"

Preston felt his muscles tremble. A sensation of sudden fear crept up upon him.

The air was tranquilly warm, stars lit the sky. Preston glanced at the determined faces of Aaron, Ashley and Kip; sensing his uneasiness they smiled warily, as they lingered outside Bennison's store. Ryan, his eyes shifting nervously, hunched up his square shoulders. The light from the store showed deep pleasure on his face. Preston jerked his head, looking suspiciously at the drunken bum turning the corner; somewhere he had seen him before. Holding a bottle possessively, he staggered blindly by, a rancid smell filling the air. There was an intense silence. A tingling sensation broke out under Preston's skin. Kip raised the brick in his hand. The clamour of breaking glass erupted through the stillness of the night. Preston followed close behind Ryan, as he found himself surrounded by liquor, cans of foods, frozen meats and rows of cookies, cartons of milk and confectionery.

He watched as they pulled down the shelves, scattering food onto the floor. He watched as they raided the store tills, pushing money into their pockets. Preston glanced around nervously. His eyes rested on a familiar stack standing in the corner of the store. With one move of his body Preston was over there, fighting desperately to free them from the cardboard box. His eyes dilated; he ripped off the ring, tilting the can to his lips, as the liquid ran down his chin. The pepsi cola, cool and tingling, entered his throat, like the spray of a fireman's hose, killing the hotness of the fire.

"Whaddya doing?" Aaron screamed, racing up to him. "You ain't got no time to drink now."

Ryan ran beside him, with scared eyes. "Take as many cans as you can Preston, then we're gonna cut and run."

Preston remained where he was. Ashley tried to heave him up. "You dumb buddy. You're suppose to be smashing up the store, not drinking trash....."

Preston felt his hair pulled sharply, a twinge of pain ran through his ears. "What's with you kid?"

"Hey you guys, leave him alone, we gotta vamoose –" Kip's shaking voice was drowned by the noise which suddenly filled the store; his mouth worked silently.

Preston's heart raced violently, his knees weakened, as he realised the alarm had gone off. Ryan's eyes were black piercing and, he had a strange look of remorse written across his darkish face. He turned and ran in the direction of his brothers. "C'mon Preston, run, it's the fuzz."

Preston thought for a moment; he looked at the can in his hand. He listened to the distant footsteps. All was silent except for the tintinnabulation of the alarm, mixed with the wail of a nearby police car. Fresh footsteps attracted Preston's ears. Car doors slammed, as the alarm suddenly stopped. The shuffling got closer. Preston tried to hide behind the stack of pepsi colas. There were audible exclamations from stalwart voices. "Well now, look at this. This sure is a pretty picture, somebody just forgot to clear the paint brushes up, that's all."

"Who would do a thing like this? It just stinks."

Preston's mind jumped involuntarily; he fought to distinguish the voices. Footsteps came closer; Preston glanced up suddenly to see the black face of a city cop, peering down at him.

"Am I seeing right, or do I need my eyes tested?" he yelled. "Kennedy, get over here."

A small explosion blasted inside Preston's head, like an electric shock. His body jolted, his eyes widened. Mr. Kennedy's leathery face wore a somewhat perplexed expression; his eyes held a familiar sternness.

"Hey kid, don't I know you?" He glanced at his partner, who shrugged his shoulders. "Are you deaf? I said, do I know you?" His voice raised to anger.

Preston felt his face grow warm, he found himself nodding his head mutely.

"Enlighten me," Mr. Kennedy persisted, "I still can't make out where I've seen that face of yours before."

Preston saw a sudden vision of the girl sitting by the cash till. She had smiled at him right here in this store. A double feeling of guilt crept up on him.

The coloured cop proceeded to drag him up. "Did you do all this here, by yourself?"

Preston shook his head.

"Wait, you dumb, can't you talk, huh?"

"Maybe." Preston tried to change his voice; fearfully he shot a glance to Mr. Kennedy. "I didn't do it all by myself, they got away I – I stayed."

"Why was that?" The coloured man averted his eyes to the can in his hand.

Mr. Kennedy screwed his blue eyes up; his finger suddenly shot out. "I know who you are – you're the boy who came by asking for Peggy, aren't you?"

A bullet went through Preston's heart. "I – I guess not."

Mr. Kennedy's arm came down swiftly. Preston dodged the blow. He felt his arm twisted from behind. "Alright – alright, I'm the guy so –"

"You know him?" the coloured man asked.

Mr. Kennedy seemed to have drifted into a daze. He nodded his head slowly. "I know him – or at least I thought I did." A gleam came into the eyes. "I looked at you back there and I thought..... hey, you don't look like a rotten J.D., but you fooled me, now I know you can't judge a book by its cover. You kids..... you're all the same, you're no different from each other."

Preston suddenly wanted to cry; he bit his lip as he thought of Peggy. It made him feel angry at his emotion, as he fought to hold back his tears, but he could not look at Mr. Kennedy any longer.

"C'mon boy" the coloured man yelled, unmoved. "Let's me and you take a ride down town." He extended his hand, pulling him through the rubble of glass, packets of food and spilled alcohol. Preston dropped the can of pepsi cola.

"You some kind of pepsi cola freak or something?" the coloured man asked sarcastically. He steered Preston to the open door of a police car.

Preston turned to stare at the man. "Yeah, I am."

He felt the hands tighten their grip on him. "You may be smart, kid, but you won't get nifty with me, hear?"

Preston was pushed on to the back seat. Beside him sat another dark-haired, burly cop. As they drove along through the inky darkness, the lit up stores, Preston closed and opened his eyes. He thought he was dreaming.

The room was cold; a naked bulb hung from the ceiling. Preston stared down at the stained, concrete floor.

"Preston..... Wildey...... King." The man with the pock-marked face, sitting on a wooden chair opposite him, was wearing a black short-sleeved, cotton shirt. He wrote down the statements in a note-book.

"Okay..... Preston, where'd you live?"

Preston raised his head. "When do I get outta here?"

"What's your phone number?"

"How long you reckon you're gonna keep me in here?"

"Listen son,..... tell me the names of the other guys."

There was a pause. Preston shrugged his shoulders.

"You won't tell me? Okay." The man rose. "See you in the morning."

The steel door swung open; the man took some keys from his waist and went out, locking the door.

Preston fractiously glanced around the claustrophobic room. In one small corner there lay a grey blanketed cot; above it hung a tiny, clouded window, suspended by bars. An up-turned wooden box, sat alongside the scratched wall. A few battered books and magazines rested on top of it.

Preston lay down on the cot, ignoring the musty smell, the stained pillow. He thought about Peggy, he thought about his mother, Erica, Mrs. Rosenberg and Ryan. He awoke sometime later, to sounds of opening doors, followed by rapid footsteps.

"Okay boy, get up, get washed, tidy this cell." Sunlight streamed in through the door. The young man, with his dimpled chin, looked down at him hard. "What number are you?"

Preston shielded his eyes. "I...... don't...... know."

"You're number 8051, so no smart games with me, okay?"

Still drugged with sleep, Preston limped along the stony corridor. His dead leg came alive as he kicked at a wall. He followed a few more dishevelled, yawning boys to the washing facilities.

"What're..... you..... in for?" a tall dark-haired boy shouted, as he washed his face under the faucet. "What're you doing time for?"

"Raiding.... a store." Preston croaked. He winced as the cold water touched his chest.

"Tall story." The boy faced him, his eyebrows raised. "You don't look the type."

The echoing sounds of boys shouting in the distance reached Preston's ears. A nostalgic feeling overcame him; it was a weird thing to be washing under different faucets.

"I mug old ladies, you know that?" The boy was rubbing a white towel over his bare chest and under his arms. "I come in and outta here, like a yo-yo." He laughed thickly, followed by a heavy smoker's cough.

Preston looked at him. His face was somewhat nondescript, his skin had the aspect of a peach. A fraternizing smile came over his lips.

"C'mon, I'll show you where we can get some gruel – you better eat it."

They sat side by side, behind a 12-seater wooden table. Boys with morose expressions sat listlessly, gazing at one another, waiting too for something to break their fast.

A moment passed. The boy picked up his pannikin, waved it in the air. "Hey we want our jarva."

There was the sound of cutlery and plates, a steady murmur of voices.

"Shuddup Jefferson, or you won't have any coffee at all." A man with a bulbous nose yelled. "You'll wait your turn."

Jefferson lowered his head, and eyed Preston thoughtfully. "The food in here is lousy crap, you gotta eat it...... or you starve."

Preston shrugged his shoulders. "What is it?"

"Mostly coffee and pancakes with maple syrup, but there ain't no bacon and eggs, no sunny side up at all man." He broke in to a short paroxysm of laughter. "It's rough inside, but you gotta hang in there babe."

Preston glanced cautiously around the huge dining hall; cold eyes stared back at him, and he felt his stomach churn. A while later, he sipped the black coffee that he wished was pepsi cola; it burned his mouth. Jefferson glanced up from his plate, and looked at Preston's plate. "You don't eat huh?"

Blowing on his coffee, Preston shook his head. He watched as Jefferson pushed his plate across the table to a sharp-featured boy.

"Maybe the rapist will eat these, they're nourishing, besides you'll need the strength for when you get outta here."

The boy raised his grey eyes. There was a callousness about them that seemed to match his fearful appearance. He shifted a shock of blond hair from his forehead. Preston thought he must be around seventeen. He felt confused about the way his heart had suddenly began to beat faster.

Jefferson's hazel eyes were watching him. He leaned closer. "The going is hard for him in here. He goes around raping anything without pants."

Preston thought; how do you know?

"In fact" Jefferson continued, his eyes getting wider, "I'm beginning to think that maybe he's a misogynist, a goddamn hater of women, you know what I mean?"

"Hell, I don't know what I'm letting myself in for, here." Preston said calmly.

Jefferson laughed. "You scared of him? Then listen, you better take a look around you, there's plenty more like him."

Preston kept his eyes fixed on Jefferson.

"There's fags, there's murderers..... and thieves and sex maniacs of all kinds, hey, I even had one guy make a pass at me."

A nervous sensation circulated through Preston's body; he wondered if his face looked as scared as he felt.

"One of these wardens with a scar on his face, he has a liking for pretty guys like us. So you better watch that little ass of yours, unless you want it tweaked."

The rest of Preston's morning was spent in interrogation. Three broad men were listlessly gazing at him from behind a dusty table. The man with the double chin held a note pad and a pen, and every answer that Preston gave, he wrote it down swiftly.

"Okay, now listen." The man in dark shades suddenly snapped them off revealing green eyes with slight bags underneath. "We have been here nearly all morning, just try..... okay I'm gonna ask you this one more time..... what made you raid Bennison's store?"

Preston raised his eyes slowly. "I told you before, I just felt like it, okay?"

"Sure it wasn't just a game of kleptomania?"

"What's that?"

"Guys just don't go around doing things because they feel like it, you know. That's more than a peccadillo."

There was a restless silence. Preston shuffled his feet impatiently. His eyes drifted to the man with bushy brows, who was watching him curiously.

"How old are you?" His voice was thin.

Preston outstretched his palm. "You've asked me that five times now."

"Okay then, tell me your full name."

Preston glanced at the wall. "I don't think I want my full name published in the paper."

"Don't worry, you won't become famous overnight."

Preston looked at him. "Preston Elvis Wildey-King."

The man nodded to the man with the double chin, who wrote it down. "Okay Preston, you ever been in a juvenile detention centre before, someplace else?..... you ever committed a crime before, ever done something offensive before? Illegal?..... you ever been on parole?"

Preston shook his head, confused.

"You have any explanation of why you done this? What are the names of the other guys? You know 'em? Are they relatives? Have you ever been in a joint before?" He paused, putting his hands beneath his chin. "You know, Preston, the sooner you answer these questions, the sooner you're gonna get outta here."

Preston blinked his eyes miserably.

"You may even have to stand trial, you know that?"

"I'll call my lawyer."

The man laughed ironically. "I never knew kids like you had lawyers. I also know that you haven't got one, and that you're liable to be in here for a long while."

A pang of fright hit Preston. He could feel the stinging of tears welling up inside his eyes. He thought angrily; I won't let this happen to me again.

He was indolent on his pallicasse cot, reading the dusty book he had found in the room, when the cell door flew open. A stalwart man, with a look of contempt in his eyes, gazed down at him.

Preston warily ran his eyes over his face. He was thinking about the warder with the scar. He sat up, closing the book.

"Number 8051, get up, you have a visitor."

A new feeling of apprehension made Preston go hot and cold; his mind slipped away to another world..... the world that was waiting for him outside. Following the man down the corridor, he came to a glass partition. With a racing heart, he saw his mother, clad in a checked shirt. She was sitting behind the glass with sad eyes. She looked up, then smiled.

"Hi, Preston you look wonderful."

Preston swallowed hard. He sat down on the wooden chair opposite her. "You too mom."

There was an awkward silence. Preston could feel his mother's eyes on him, and tried to avoid them.

"What – what made you do it Preston?"

He glanced up, noticing her wavering voice. "What made me do it?..... I don't know."

Preston watched, as she fumbled inside her purse. She pulled out a packet of West Virginias, glanced around, then put them back furtively in her purse.

"Where's Erica...... isn't she gonna visit me? Not that I want her to."

Mrs. Wildey-King tossed her hair back. "She's staying at Alma O'Neal's house for two days, working on some assignments."

Preston shrugged. "She's always doing that."

His mother leaned closer to the glass. "How you doing in here, is it alright?"

"It's pretty noisy..... the place is like a prison camp."

"I brought some of your clothes. I gave them to one of those warders, he'll send them down to you."

Preston glanced at her.

"What's the food like?" Her dark eyes wandered over him. "Are you eating?"

Preston shrugged. "You got any pepsi cola on you?"

Her face shadowed "You can't do without that stuff can you? Is that the reason why you broke in the store?"

A hot sweat crept up on Preston's back. "What do you think?"

Her eyes widened; she shook her head. "I think Preston...... that..... you are slowly going out of your mind..... crazy, that's what I think."

Preston felt the muscles of his face tighten. "That supposed to be some kind of compliment?"

She flashed him an angry look. "No, a slip of the tongue. I don't know how to make you feel sorry for what you've done Preston. If your father was here he'd –"

"He's not here, so don't talk about him."

Her eyes were stern, her expression puzzled. "Don't you feel guilty of what you've done? Of what you're putting me through when you act this way? Don't you have thoughts for anybody but yourself?"

Preston glanced away. He clenched his jaws, trying to restrain the lump in his throat at the same time.

"Don't look away –"

"Listen, I'll be out of here before you know it."

"I don't care when you come out." Her voice rose. "You ought to stay in here until you learn to feel guilty. It's the thought about what you're gonna do when you get out that gets me, are you gonna raid another store, huh?"

A few other visitors were watching them. A coloured warder signalled over to them to lower their voices.

Mrs. Wildey-King kept her eyes fixed on Preston. Preston stared back passively. "So you don't like the way I behave. Did you wait for me to come in here, to tell me that?" His voice was shaking.

She looked away. "You make me sick."

Preston bit his lip. "I thought so. Then that makes two of us."

The bell system rang. Preston got up abruptly, turned to the door and walked rapidly back to his room.

Sixteen boys were trying to start a game of basket-ball. The sun was like a fire-ball in the sky. Preston strolled desolately on to the concrete recess ground.

"C'mon, Pittsburg, stack-house, Anderson, get those feet up. Get some air into you, let's see you move...... c'mon, I wanna see you run like the devil's after you. I wanna see that ball fly in the air......."

A tall, close cropped man, clad in a bright orange track-suit, was yelling out, jumping up and down. He caught the ball, bounced it, then threw it unexpectedly at the group of huddled boys.

"...... Miller...... Kaminski, the ball ain't gonna come to you. What are you standing dreaming for Jackson? What'd you say Tomplin? No you can't drop out. Nor you Homburg, so get your tail right back here..... I thought I told you to go to the john before Otter...... pass the ball over that way. C'mon I don't wanna see you all dry up. I wanna see you sweat it out......I wanna hear the rhythm of that bounce. Don't go around chasing one another..... c'mon you crazy punks, move, keep the ball rolling. Ain't no time to tie your laces up now Scobie.... Scobie you hear me?..... I wanna see you pant like a dawg Mclask..... Okay everybody..... stop..... stop." The whistle blew shrilly.

Preston felt a hand on his shoulder. He smiled; it was Jefferson.

"How you doing kid?" He dug out a packet of cigarettes from his shirt pocket. "You smoke?"

Preston glanced at him. He took a cigarette reluctantly. "You have a light?" Jefferson opened up a silver, compact case; a spear of fire slowly emerged. "That's a beauty, where'd you get it?"

"Hussled it." Jefferson examined the lighter in his hand. "One of my best catches, you know."

Preston looked at him, inhaling his cigarette vigorously.

"You wanna get outta this lousy slammer?" He asked after a while.

Tilting the cigarette from his mouth, Preston raised his eyes. "You know how to?"

Jefferson looked away toward a barbed-wired fence. "It'll cost you."

The air was filled with loud shouts. The man in the track-suit was surrounded by boys, shouting to a boy with flossy hair, who was bouncing the ball off the pitch. "You see what's behind that fence? That's the girls' joint." Jefferson pointed his arm. "See along, behind those trash cans, there's a hole about six inches wide. I tried getting through, with this guy named Shadrack. I was caught, he got away, but he was caught seven hours later. Dig that?"

Preston scrutinised the fence. "Maybe but – "

"I ain't trying to syke you out, but you can try."

"Hey listen, I'll get caught. I'll do time." Preston glanced at Jefferson. "What good is that, huh?"

He shrugged nonchalantly, drew his cigarette. "Maybe you won't, anyway what're you, a jail-house punk?"

Preston stubbed out his cigarette on the wall. "I don't know. This place is more like a freedom-school, than a pen."

Jefferson suddenly laughed. "You've only been here two days. You sure have got a lot of living to do, but right now you're just living it off the wall."

Preston glanced away. "You mean putting that nine to five on the shelf, right?"

"Sure, that's right." Jefferson turned him around. "I only know your number, what's your name kid?"

"Preston."

Jefferson shook his head. "Preston..... you're a million laughs, welcome to the clan."

They were washing sheets in the laundry the next day. The place was filled with the sounds of oscillating washing machines. A vapour of steam rose into the air. An obscure curtain enveloped the spacious room.

Preston worked strenuously, folding the wet linen, piling it on top of other washed linen. He glanced at Jefferson, who was hauling a sheet from the machine. His face was perspiring; the biceps on his arms swelled out more prominently. Standing a distance away was the supervisor, his arms folded against his chest. Preston could feel his eyes on him. He glanced at him hotly, in hope that he would notice how hard he was working. He was thinking about what he'd do once he was out of here. He'd forget about a few things, start anew, work hard at his studies. He'd show his mother what he could do, he wasn't going to be a failure. Maybe he'd find a way to win Peggy back, sitting in the park, telling each other their dreams. Maybe they'd marry someday..... Preston's mouth felt suddenly dry. He pulled the sheet to his face, sucking it urgently, hoping it would relieve him from his thirstiness. Jefferson, with a tray of folded sheets, staggered past him. "I've finished," he yelled above the stentorian noise. "I'll see you in the recreation room, okay?" Preston watched him disappear in the haze of steam, and turned back to the machine, patiently awaiting his next batch of sheets.

The supervisor caught his eye, and walked a few inches in his direction. "King, get your back in that work and quit looking like you wanna visit the john." His voice reverberated above the noisy machines. "You have about fifteen minutes left, and I'll have you know that you're not going anywhere until you finished that, hear?"

Preston peeked in through the glass window of the machine; it looked like two more sheets to go. He suddenly realised how tired he was, his back was aching.

"Hey, can I help you any?" Preston slowly turned around. His gaze met a tall, coloured boy, with high afro hair. He was smiling, revealing large white teeth; his eyes were huge, stern and black. Sweat poured down his face. "You really are in a tangle here." He helped, as Preston turned to drag the sheet out. He proceeded to take one end, together they rotated it in time to the hum of the mangle.

A moment passed. Preston glanced up; he felt a sudden revulsion, as he noticed the boy still smiling strangely.

"What're you doing time for? You know why I'm here?" He spoke suddenly, leaning down to wipe the sweat on his forearm. "I go round knifing people. My name's White." Preston stopped. He stared at him, an apprehensive feeling coming over him. He found his eyes wandering nervously. "They'd put me in the electric chair if they could, but they're too scared." The boy dropped his side of the sheets. "They're only locking me up 'cause I'm black, they wouldn't do that to you, you're white. You're bright, you have it made."

Preston tensed, he tried to smile.

"Yeah, you lovely, blue eyed ice-berg, nobody can touch you." He pointed to a deep scar on his arm. "Look, they even torture me – listen you nigger, they say, you better tell us the truth or we're gonna cut you up to shreds. Then they slash at me." He bent down swiftly to his sneakers. "I'll show you."

Preston averted his eyes to the supervisor. He was standing with his back to them. When he glanced at the boy again, his heart jumped. He was brandishing a shining blade.

"Look at this." He waved it in front of him. "This is the blade that I use on them too – I cut them up too."

"Who are they?" Preston's voice began to shake. "Who are the guys you cut up?"

The boy's eyes seemed remote. "You wouldn't believe how many – this blade cut up more people than you'd believe. Last month I had my twentieth victim."

"Who are you – the second son of Sam?"

A gleam came into his eyes. "Of course not, man, they call me midnight. You know why, cause I go round seeking these people when the moon is bright, and my seeing is right." He laughed wheezily.

For a while they stared at each other. Seriously. Sombrely.

The boy suddenly tilted the blade to Preston's chin. "Don't move one little bit."

A cold sensation travelled through Preston's body. He imagined himself lying in a pool of blood. A mutilated corpse, left lying in a jail house laundry. He turned his head. "Get out of my way, you want me to call the supervisor?"

"Uh-oh you've already done that." Preston felt the pressure of his hand on his throat. "Little, white sucker, you're a dead man."

A sharp, stinging sensation occurred on Preston's left jaw-bone; he glanced shakily at the blade. It wore blood. Before the blade moved, he found new strength. He lashed out at the boy's face, hoping to make him drop the blade. There was a loud shout of anger; Preston, grabbing hold of the boy's shirt, realised it was his own voice.

There was a sound of running feet. The supervisor was upon them, separating them. "What's all the shouting about? Whyn't you working White? Get back to your own section, now move it."

Preston watched anxiously as the coloured boy stepped forward, his teeth shining. "Yes suh, nice suh, sorry suh." His arm moved swiftly. The supervisor doubled over, his face contorted, his eyes protruding and he clutched at the sheet in Preston's hands.

The boy bent over. He pulled the blade out from the man's reddened tee shirt. Preston watched as he collapsed onto the floor, the white sheet crimsoned to a bright glistening pattern. Two blue eyes stared up at him. Preston looked away. He looked at the coloured boy. The boy looked back.

"He's my twenty-first victim." The boy kicked out at him. "And you're my next, you better not run."

A short silence. Preston stared at the bloodied blade. Thoughts ran through his mind, thoughts that seemed to enliven his brain. With an impulsive jerk, he raised his leg, aiming at the boy's hand. The blade fell sharply to the floor. The boy moved; Preston impetuously ran in to him, bringing them both to the floor. An arm lashed out, Preston felt his nose burn, he tasted blood.

White's fists were flying madly, his eyes were fiery. Preston felt the wet sheet as he fell back. He raised both legs, letting his arm wander the floor for the blade. He grabbed a slimy hand, let go, then felt the blade. White was suddenly on top of him. There was a stiffening pull, and the blade was in his hand. The machines had stopped, the air was filled with shouts and running feet, getting closer all the time. Preston suddenly felt White's body get lighter. Two arms were dragging him up. The blade fell swiftly onto Preston's exposed chest. He clamped his hand on it, as a small sting ran through him.

"Hey what goes on here?" A boy with blond hair was helping him up.

"What happened here?"

Preston kept his gaze fixed on White. He was looking at him with enmity in his eyes.

"This guy's dead." A boy raised his blood covered hand toward the rest of the wide-eyed assembled boys. "He's been stabbed –"

"Okay, what's the story in here?" A man in black charged through the motionless boys. In his hand was a six-shooter gun. His eyes fell on the corpse. "Okay, freeze, the lot of you."

More policemen arrived on the scene, each one brandishing a gun, each one looking at the motionless man, entangled in a bloodied sheet.

"Which one of you is responsible for this?" The man's eyes drifted from White's to Preston. Preston glanced at his clammy hand; it was red with blood, blood that came from the dead man. A wave of nausea, a convulsive twitch; Preston saw the ground rush up to him.

He was in his cell, lying on his cot, floating on a sea of pepsi cola. The bulb swayed dizzily above him. Preston felt too exhausted to sit up. He closed his eyes, his mind drifting away from him. He was in a small tavern. People were drinking from small yellow glasses. A man with an oval shaped head came forward holding a can of pepsi cola; he tossed it playfully to another man, who threw it to a woman. Preston was feeling a little annoyed, he wanted the pepsi cola for himself. He recognised his own voice as he shouted out.

The man who had started the game clamped a hand on his shoulder, shaking him harshly. "There is no pepsi cola, now c'mon, wake up."

The voice echoed, Preston opened his eyes. A different man was peering down at him. "Hey kid, are you alright now?"

Preston felt a cold dampness around him; he glanced downwards. The comforters on his cot were sliding down on the floor. He was wearing nothing, apart from his under-pants.

"You look kinda delirious, you know." The man was smiling almost smugly. "I never knew you liked pepsi cola so much."

Preston weakly tried to drag the comforters back to help him, until the comforter was cosily wrapped around him.

"What.... time..... is it?" Preston felt the warmness creep back into him.

"Just gone midnight, you've missed your chuck."

There was something about him that seemed familiar. Preston suddenly remembered where he was. "What..... happened...... to..... White?"

The man slowly rubbed his hand alongside Preston's leg. "Relax..... he's been transferred to another joint..... you're in the clear..... now get some sleep."

Preston closed his heavy eyes. A moment later he heard the clank of his cell door slamming. The keys turned, the footsteps hurried away. Preston's eyes flew open. He sat up shakily, suddenly remembering Jefferson's words; "Beware of the warder with the scar on his face." The man had just been in here.

"C'mon I want this floor cleaned," a man's voice rang out. "I want this floor to sparkle. I want it scrubbed, like you never scrubbed before."

Carrying his bucket and brush to the end of the corridor, Preston knelt down on the stony floor. He dipped the brush scornfully into the disinfectant water. The sounds of the other boys scrubbing seemed to make the delinquent centre come alive.

"Taylor, you want any line on how to do the job properly?" the man yelled again. He flipped his fingers. "Then do it right, huh?"

Preston scrubbed strenuously; his throat became dry. Footsteps sounded. He glanced up. Two men were talking. The other coloured supervisor stared down at him. "King? 8051? Okay move, you have a visitor."

Preston felt an abrupt feeling of uneasiness. He rose, leaving the other boys scrubbing; they glanced up at him as he went by.

"You know who it is?" he asked, following the young supervisor down an empty corridor.

The man shrugged his wide shoulders. "I don't know. It's a lady, could be your mother."

Preston's eyes dropped. "What does she look like?"

"Brunette..... tall, slim." He gesticulated his hands. "Wearing a beige blouse, looks young."

"Then it can't be my mom, she's not a brunette."

The supervisor laughed, and quickened his pace. "Who might it be then, your girlfriend?"

A series of thoughts rushed through Preston's mind. His heart raced, he was thinking of Peggy. They pushed open the door and the supervisor directed him to the glass partition. As Preston saw the tall brunette sitting opposite the glass, his heart somersaulted. Her hair was high in a chignon; she smiled affectionately as their eyes met. Preston sat down. "Hi Mrs. Rosenberg."

Her eyes behind her glasses enlarged. "It's good to see you Preston."

For a moment, they gazed at each other. Preston began to feel slightly embarrassed at his position.

"You know something, you really scared me, when I found out you were here." Her voice was soft. "I really don't understand it at all."

Preston glanced away.

"Where did you get that cut on your chin?"

He looked up. "You missed me, I guess...... I missed you."

She smiled coyly. "Of course I missed you, I couldn't get to sleep at nights."

"Listen Connie." Preston felt penitence arouse in him. "I'm kinda sorry, it had to be this way."

She looked suddenly hurt. "I just take things as they come. I don't care what you do..... I just wish we were together."

Preston shrugged, bewildered. "But we are."

Her eye-brows raised. "We can't even touch one another Preston. You look so beautiful on the other side of this glass."

He felt a warmness spread over his face. He looked at her. "I think you look better with your hair down and you look different without your glasses."

"Oh you think so?" Her hand flew to her head. "I'm always putting my hair like this." Preston watched as she tilted her head, letting her hair loose like a running waterfall. She took her glasses off. "I'm doing this all for you."

"You look wonderful...... Connie I still love you too."

She nodded her head absently. "You love me, I love you and – and I think I'm gonna cry Preston." She lowered her eyes.

Preston felt a fearsome curiosity boil up inside him; he stared at her perplexed. "What's the matter? Why are you gonna cry? I'll be out of here soon."

She looked up, her eyes swelling with tears, shaking her head. "It's not that Preston. I'm leaving you."

Preston's stomach sunk, his heart began to thump. "Connie, leaving me?"

She stared at him intensely. "Leif is back from Europe." She spoke quietly. "And....... he's just back."

"Your husband's back, so you're leaving me?" Preston had a sudden vision of a dark-haired broad man.

"I'm leaving you Preston – I'm leaving because Leif has bought us a house someplace in Europe." She raised her hand to the glass. "You understand? I have to go."

Preston watched as the tears poured openly down her face. He shrugged his shoulders feeling lost. "I don't know what to say. What can I say?"

"..... That you love me..... and that you always will, no matter what." She made an attempt to smile through her tears. "Come what may."

Preston felt his jaw tremble. "How – how can I love you, when you'll be a million miles away? Connie – don't do this to me."

She outlined his face on the glass. "Don't give me a hard time babe, of course you'll love me. It has to be that way."

Preston turned away. "If you loved your husband, then why did I ever get caught up with you? You knew all along – you knew all along that you were gonna leave to Europe. You just wanted someone to keep you company, till he got back."

"That's not true, you're talking as though it's my fault Preston." She choked. "I didn't ask him to come home early. I didn't ask him to buy a goddamned house in Europe. So quit making it like I'm the one who wants to go."

Preston felt the tears well up. He looked at her levelly. "Then why go huh?"

"Don't cry, please don't cry." She leaned closer to the glass, kissing it as though it were Preston. "I love you. I mean that. I didn't want to hurt you so."

Preston watched as she rose; he tried to talk. He wanted to say, can't you just wait until I get out of here?

"So long Preston, you'll be in my heart always." She turned sharply away, walking across the room, getting faster all the time.

Preston watched her figure disappear behind swing doors. With one hand concealing his wet eyes, he walked out the room, as the visitors' bell rung at four o'clock.

He was thinking about what he'd do when he got out of here. He'd forget about Mrs. Rosenberg, he'd start his life over again......

"How'd it go then, was it your mother?" The supervisor ambled beside him. "Hey, are you crying?.....

I can tell you, she looked more like your girlfriend than your mother."

Preston scrubbed hard with his brush on the floor. He slowly felt his anger ebb away. For a moment he wondered why his tears would not cease, then he realised his heart had just been broken.

The aroma of beef stew, drifting around the large dining hall, did not do anything to increase Preston's hunger. He watched morbidly as boys held out their plates to be served. Jefferson was at the back of him, waiting patiently for him to make up his mind. He glanced at the middle-aged man, then at the soggy stew in the bowl. "I don't think I can eat any of that stuff."

The pock faced man raised a spoon of stew to his nose. "This ain't just stuff, that is food, try some."

Preston felt Jefferson prod him in the ribs. "It may taste like leather, Preston, but you better eat it or you'll starve."

Preston shrugged his shoulders. "I'm not hungry." He turned away, his eyes meeting a supervisor. The man clamped a hand on his shoulder. "King, you better eat that food now." His voice was harsh. "If you're going on a hunger strike, I can force feed you."

"You can't do that."

The supervisor stared at him. "I don't want you walking outta here like a bean-pole. Your folks'll think we don't feed you in here, but we do, and plenty."

Preston felt a sickly juice form in his mouth, as the supervisor steered him back to the counter. He watched as the stew was slumped on to a plate. All the frustration, all the anger that he'd bottled up inside him, came crashing out. At an impulse, Preston snatched the plate high above his head, and brought it down with a sharp crash to the floor. He was surprised. "I don't want no goddamn stew okay?"

Jefferson backed away, his mouth open. The man in white gazed down at the stew, as though he'd lost something valuable. The supervisor's face strangely contorted, he raised his hands calmly. "Okay, okay, take it –"

"Shut up, just shut up about that." Preston yelled; he was beginning to feel good.

"You think you can make me do everything. You think you can make me eat things I don't like."

There was a loud roar of approval, followed by a light round of applause. The other thousand, eating boys, were amused at the commotion.

Preston felt suddenly dazed with fright. He watched as a long-haired boy jumped on a table, holding his plate high. "Yeah, you tell 'em, you tell everybody what's right."

Another chorus of approval rose from the boys, followed by stamping feet, smashing of plates, and the sound of bells as boys banged their cutlery on the tables. Preston turned. Jefferson was shouting above the turmoil.

"Hey, you've really rocked it now......"

Policemen in black were charging in, brandishing guns, supervisors tried vainly to restrain the unruly boys. Preston suddenly wanted to get away. A sharp crack sounded in the resonant room. "Now quit the noise, all of you." A policeman stood audaciously on a table, a gun waving in the air. "I'll shoot again if I have to, and this time it's gonna be one of you guys." The noise continued, growing louder all the while. Another crack sounded, and the noise began to subside.

"Just shut up, sit up and eat up, or there's gonna be big trouble."

Preston charged through a line of boys. Running rapidly, avoiding supervisors as they tried to catch him, he raced through the hall. In his mind was a row of faces, one was Mrs. Rosenberg's, the other Peggy's. He ran through the swing doors, the breeze blowing around his burning face. Down the left corridor, up the right corridor, boys were leaning on the walls; Preston felt lost. He turned, imagining he was racing against the wind. The thought of his suffocating cell made him change direction, and he headed for the recess ground. Panting now, Preston was relieved to inhale fresh air, and the sun greeted him hotly. His mind became clear, anger ceased, anxiety took over. He paced the ground, wondering if he would have a chance to feel feminine skin in his arms again. Realising his powerful urge for female comfort, a pang of fright hit him. If he was like this at fourteen, then what sort of man would he be at forty?

On an impulse he raced to his cell. Flicking through the dusty magazines left behind by some other guy, Preston relaxed on his cot. A quiver ran through him, and he felt a sharp pull between his legs, as he eyed the page of naked girls. A moment of excitement passed; Preston stroked his genitals rhythmically, a warmth of security crept over him. He closed his eyes. A moment later, his cell door flew open. Preston jerked up, slipping the magazine under his pillow. He raised his eyes. The supervisor from the dining hall was staring at him, a strange light in his grey eyes.

"Wildey-King, owing to your obstreperous behaviour back there, which led to violence, I have been ordered to take you down for hard labour."

Preston shrugged his shoulders sheepishly. "Okay....."

It was his fourteenth day in endurance. Preston threw the ball to Jefferson in the yard. "Hey let me do it huh, I'll show you how."

The sun was hot on Preston's back, and his white tee shirt clung to him with perspiration. He watched as Jefferson bounced the ball, to the game of twenty one. A long while passed.

"Hey Preston, guess what, I'm having out." Jefferson glanced at him, bouncing the ball. "Tomorrow sometime."

Envy rose in Preston. "How long you been in here?"

The sound of bumps against the wall. "I don't know..... maybe half a year or so."

"What're you gonna do when you get out?"

"What, get outta here?..... I don't know, hang out with the guys, I guess."

Preston glanced at him. "You like coming in here."

He stopped the ball suddenly, his eyes dreamy. "It's my home really – my folks are dead. I got no brothers or sisters. I live with this wise old lady, I call aunty." His face changed. "What're you gonna do when you get out of here?"

"I don't know..... just live I guess."

Jefferson nodded his head compatibly, the ball resting on his chest. "Just live, I kinda like that." He swiped at the air with his free arm. "I mean what else is there to do, huh?"

Preston shrugged, shifting the hair from his eyes. "I don't know....." He was thinking seriously of what he'd like to do. His eyes met Jefferson's. "Hey what is your name?"

"How do you mean?" He laughed abruptly. "The name's Jefferson."

"That isn't your first name is it?"

"Don't you like it?" His brows shot up. "That's the name everybody calls me, besides I'm pretty used to it now. My first name's Marshall."

Preston smirked. "I dig that..... knew a girl called Marcia, in kindergarten. Use to call her marsh-mallow."

"Say..... that's cute." He tossed his long hair. "Do I remind you of her?"

Preston felt his face glow. "Not exactly.... uh-uh, she was much too pretty."

"You know something, you remind me of a cup-cake." Jefferson's expression had changed to affection. He threw his arm limply across Preston. "I like cup-cakes and I like you. Don't ask me why, but I do."

He was washing his face one morning, two days later; the water from the faucet was ice-cold. Pulling some paper from the roll towel, Preston noticed one of the warders looking at him curiously. He turned off the faucet as he heard the man come up behind him. "How you doing boy?" His voice was soft. "Alright, you're not lonesome or anything?"

Preston turned to glance at him. He had an English hair-cut, and his blond moustache was trimmed neatly below his small nose. "I'm fine."

"I hope so." He seemed anxious. "I'm always around..... if you ever feel you need to talk to somebody..... I'm..... you're welcome, okay?"

Preston lowered his eyes, feeling suddenly awkward. He made a pretence of wiping his hands.

"I hear your friend has left us; did you like him?"

A vision of Jefferson came into Preston's mind. He raised his eyes. "Yeah, he was alright."

The man's sharp eyes strayed over him. "Good. I liked him too. He liked me....."

Preston suddenly conscious of his bare chest, swept his eyes over to his tee shirt, resting on a nearby chair. The man, catching his glance, turned and handed him the tee shirt. "You ought to eat the food in here." His hand shot out. "I can just about see your ribs. I can feel them too."

Preston noticed his tone of anger; he was aware of the silence that reigned in the washroom. He flinched away, pulling on his tee shirt.

The man stared at him, a light passing his eyes. "Why don't you eat, huh?....." He stepped forward. "Listen, I don't like skinny boys. I don't like boys with no flesh on them. I like them....."

Knocking against the wall, Preston was forced to stop. He calmly eyed the man's outstretched hands; they were large, each one was covered with long scratch marks. "Don't...... be...... afraid, I only want to whisper something in your ear." His face was beaded with sweat.

"Like what, huh?" Preston's eyes darted to the entrance of the wash-room.

"Like, are you scared of the dark?"

"Are you crazy? Course not."

"Tell me you are. Tell me that you need a kiss and cuddle before you go to sleep."

Preston shook his head, confused, his heart palpitating; he inhaled the man's strong after-shave.

"Wouldn't you like to sleep in my room tonight? I get lonesome too, you know."

"I'll see you around, huh." Preston made an attempt to move. He felt the man's hand push against his chest.

"I wanna see you now, so cut that talk out. You're going nowhere." A smile passed his thin lips. "Not until I finish with you, anyway."

Three boys swaggered in to the room. Preston watched apprehensively as the man suddenly withdrew. The boys, each with long hair, were talking, seeming unaware of what was going on.

Preston inched toward the entrance. The man stood there for a moment, his hand dangling the keys on his hip. "Okay boys," he yelled. "Let's go get our breakfast."

Preston raced down the corridor. The loud hum of boys talking filled his ears as he entered the large canteen.

The sun scorched down through the windows of the recreation room. Preston shifted uncomfortably in the red foamed divan, trying vainly to listen to the television show. A few boys were seated around an oblong table, shouting out remarks as they indulged in a game of crap. A crowd of impatient boys watched eagerly as two opponents stretched across a pool table, their arms at the ready to strike.

Preston's eyes drifted over to the muscular supervisor; he was headed toward him. "Follow me kid, you have a visitor."

He rose quickly and followed him through the corridor, his heart racing so that his temples began to throb. When he spotted Peggy, clad in a turquoise tee shirt, behind the glass, his stomach suddenly went hollow. She smiled. Preston, looking at her levelly, noticed a look of impatience about her face. He sat down, all his hopes beginning to fade.

"Hi Preston, long time no see."

Preston tried to sound nonchalant. "…..That's supposed to be my line."

"So I see, I never realised you wanted to care." There was a hint of sarcasm in her melodious voice. Preston, searching for words, avoided her eyes. He looked across at another conversing couple, trying hard to hear what they were saying. "Hey listen….. I came here for a reason you know, to talk."

"So, talk."

She sighed impatiently. "You look like a toilet, and you stink worse, you know that?"

Preston flashed her a look of annoyance. "So, is that what you came here to talk about?"

Her lips formed into a furtive smile. "No….. actually I came to say goodbye."

Preston drew a deep breath. "Thanks for enlightening me."

"Hey you forget that you slept off on me at that cafeteria?" Her voice rose in anger. "So what do you expect me to say, huh?"

A feeling of guilt hovered over Preston; he glanced away.

"Maybe you'd like to think that I didn't recognise it. That I appreciated it. Who do you take me for, one of your good-time girls? I'm just not cut out for that."

There was a painful silence. A stream of sunlight attacked the dusty air through a small cracked window. Peggy put one side of her shining hair behind her ear. "Okay….. look I'm sorry…… sorry for us……sorry that we didn't work out okay."

Preston shrugged. He felt a sensation that he'd never felt before. Impotence mixed with passion, with anger. "You don't have to say you're sorry."

"I'm getting tired of you Preston." Her voice seemed accusing. "How many more times are you gonna raid stores? How many more times do I have to stand by you in situations like this, huh?"

"Listen, I didn't ask you to stand –"

"Shut-up, shut-up. I don't wanna know any more okay?"

Preston, his jaws clenched, glanced away to the large clock on the wall. It read ten of three. Every person in the room seemed to be waiting, waiting for their loud conversation to go on.

"Preston." Peggy's voice was low, with anxiety. "What's happened to us?"

"I don't know." Preston cupped his face in his hands. "Maybe we just stopped ticking."

"Maybe." As their eyes began to lock, Preston felt a strange urge to pull away.

"So, you're through with me?"

She hesitated for a while. For a moment her expression softened, then her eyes flared. "I'm through with you, and this time it's for real. Go have hang-ups about other girls. I just don't care any more okay?"

Preston let go his drawn breath. "Okay I'll do that. You can go have your flings with Curt Miller, I don't care anymore. I got other things to cry about."

Her face changed. "You really mean that?"

"I mean that." Preston tried to keep his voice from breaking. "Don't say you're sorry, 'cause I'm tired of people telling me that."

"What – what am I supposed to say then, that I still love you?"

Preston glanced at her suspiciously. "Did I ask you to say that?"

"No."

"Then don' t say that." For a moment they stared at one another. Peggy bit her lower lip. "But the only trouble is that I do Preston." She seemed almost mollified. "I still feel something for you."

Preston felt agitation rising in his brain. "Hey, I feel like hitting somebody, Peggy, I don't understand you. First you say you're through with me, then you say you love me. What am I supposed to believe? What's with you, huh?"

She shook her head, her cheeks crimsoning. "I don't know. Why'd I ever come here at all?"

"Don't – don't come back here again."

"Don't worry, I won't." Her tone was sardonic. Her eyes glistened.

The bell rang. Preston turned cold. Looking at her, he realised with some anger that he still desired to throw his arms around her and kiss her. She rose unsteadily, her hair shielding her face. "Goodbye Preston."

His throat tightened. He watched as she turned sharply away. Somewhere at the back of his mind he had a feeling that this had happened before. He remained seated, his head in his hands. A tiny voice, calling from within his heart said; "I'm betting westerns will be back and so will you."

Three days later a paternal looking man with a paunchy stomach was sitting opposite him. Preston glanced around the dusty, shady room.

"Right, King." The man rustled a bunch of papers. "I want a few details from you. What are the names of the guys who helped you raid that store?"

Preston tensed. "Supposing I don't know them?"

"I'd take it as an attempt to shield somebody that you don't wanna report. Right?"

Preston shrugged. "I don't know."

"You don't know what?" The man leaned over the table. "Who the guys are? What their names are, huh?"

A pang of guilt mixed with fear travelled through Preston's mind.

"I have other boys to question, you gonna tell me now?"

"I don't know them."

The man sighed. "Is that you final word? We're gonna catch the guys with your help, or without it, you know that?"

Preston lowered his eyes.

"You're gonna get off light this time boy, next time you won't be so lucky."

Preston eyed the wall continuously. There was a frame mark of a picture. He wondered what picture would have hung there.

There was a moment's silence, as the man wrote down on the paper; he glanced up. "Okay, you can go now." He paused. "We'll let you know what's gonna happen to you..... go on, go to your cell."

Feeling relieved, Preston rose stiffly from the wooden chair; he opened the door, closing it behind him. As he walked back to his cell, he painfully began to think about Ryan Kassick.

He was in his cot, with his eyes opened. The clanging of keys, followed by foot-steps, reached his ears. He stirred weakly; another day had begun. Rolling over, he wanted to go right back to sleep. His cell door flew open. Preston jerked up. A crack of sunlight blasted his eyes as he tried to focus on the warder's face.

"Okay, 8501, get up and get moving."

Preston blinked twice. "Where.... to? Am....... I gonna be....... questioned again?"

The man stepped forward; he smiled sarcastically. "No, you're getting outta here. That's where you're headed, now move."

His stomach bowled over in surprise. "I'm getting outta here, how come?"

"Don't ask any questions. Your old lady's waiting for you." He pointed a large finger. "Take care, I don't wanna see you in here ever, okay?"

As he left, Preston jumped to the ground, his heart racing with sudden happiness. His mother was standing by the entrance of the centre, her face slightly pinched. "Hi Preston..... you okay?"

Preston threw his holdall on his back. "I'm fine, and hey, it's good to see you."

She smiled anxiously at him, as he climbed in the front seat of the white Mercedes automobile. It accelerated down the wide high-way, leaving the juvenile hall remote and solitary. For a long while they did not converse. Preston began to feel awkward, upbraided, as he gazed out at the passing scenery. He found his burst of happiness suddenly diminishing when his mind remembered Mrs. Rosenberg. All his past came hurtling back to him; it shook him. For some reason, he felt like an ex-convict coming back to town.

Mrs. Wildey-King slowed down at the intersection. His eyes suddenly transfixed to the side-window. A blonde-haired petite girl was ambling along the side-walk; beside her was a tall dark-haired boy, who was talking, laughing and gesticulating. Preston felt suddenly distraught. His mother, sensing his stare, glanced cautiously in his direction. "Wasn't that Peggy back there?" She checked the rear mirror. Preston turned away, he shrugged. "I don't know..... I think so."

"You and her are still friends, I guess. Did she visit back at the centre?"

Preston eyed the dash board. "Listen mom, everything's okay between us."

"I never said it wasn't." She increased the speed. "How come you don't bring her to the apartment any more?"

He took a deep breath. "Hey, this is beginning to sound like an interrogation, you know that? I bring her when I want okay?"

A breeze of morning wind drifted through the open window. Preston closed his eyes as it swept through his hair.

"Something bugging you Preston?"

"Like what, huh?" He leaned back, trying to listen to the sound of the ground swishing beneath the smooth wheels. The tension began to mount; Peggy came into his thoughts again; he opened his eyes. They were now nearing the city centre. Preston threw his hand to the door as they rounded a corner.

"Slow down, I wanna get out and walk."

Mrs. Wildey-King gave him a bewildered glance. The automobile gradually dropped its speed. It stopped, the meter still clicking. "Why get out here?" She turned to face him. "We're almost home now."

"So, you'll see me at home later, right?" Preston leaned forward and climbed out, slamming the door shut. For a moment his mother stared at him through the glass, then she pressed her foot down, speeding away down the alley.

Preston remained still for a while. He scanned the area, suddenly feeling overwhelmed with his freedom. The sun was already shining strongly, from a cloudless sky. Sea-gulls flapped their wings like dried paper, around the cerulean river, which receded in delicate waves. Preston peered into the lucid water; his reflection stared back at him. A few straggling people ambled by on the bridge above. One of them was a blonde-haired girl who stopped to look down at the river. Preston stared up at her. His heart raced, he headed in her direction. "Hey Peggy, wait a moment."

The girl appeared not to hear. She turned away, mingling into a crowd of passers-by. Increasing his speed, Preston reached the bridge; he raced across the street, catching sight of her. For a moment he thought he was seeing Charlene Tilton, of 'Dallas', as she swung along the side-walk in a haughty fashion.

A moment later, he swung her round. "Peggy?" He stared at her in amazement. She had the mature face of a woman, and her eyes were laid out in heavy make-up. She too looked surprised. "Hey, what is this, day light attack?"

Preston dropped his hand from her shoulder. "I'm sorry I thought you were somebody else."

The woman looked him up and down. "You're only a boy too. I ought to report –"

"Listen, it was a mistake." Preston backed away. "I didn't mean anything okay?"

The street seemed suddenly quiet. Hunching his shoulders, hands in pockets, Preston strode back up the side-walk. A feeling of despondency came over him. He glanced back at the woman; for a long while he stood there watching her walk away.

The sun was fading into an overall gloom. The beach was still crowded with the people who had left their homes since morning to celebrate Independence Day. Preston, still from lying down on the sand all day, rose slowly. He pulled on his rainbow tee shirt, picked up his last can of pepsi, and turned away from the sea.

A slight, catching breeze blew refreshingly across his forehead, parting his hair swiftly. People, energetically, were playing baseball. Preston sipped his pepsi cola. His eyes searched through the crowds vainly for Peggy. An aroma of smokey steak drifted in the air; a middle-aged couple were bent over a barbecue stand. Nearby a group of girls were prancing around after a yellow beach-ball. Preston strolled away from the beach.

Mrs. Rosenberg's house looked forlorn, rejected, as Preston approached it. He ascended the familiar steps with pangs of sorrow, as he remembered the evenings he had shared with her. The golden brass knocker stared back at him. For a moment he was seized with a sudden desire to knock it, hoping that Mrs. Rosenberg would be standing there with a smile on her face. Peeking through the drapeless windows, Preston felt a mild sensation of anger, as he stared at the bare floorboards, the picture-free walls, the empty book case. No sound of low music drifted to his ears this time, no bitter tasting wine made his eyes dilate, no trembling sensations, as he remembered how amorously entwined he had sat through the night with his own teacher. He bit his lip. Holding back his tears he closed his eyes tight, imagining that for one moment he was with her.

Deep in a trance, Preston heard a door open. He glanced up, his eyes straying to the next house. A red-haired, stout woman was staring at him from behind a tall broomstick. "What can I do for you son?..... if you're looking for Mrs. Rosenberg, she doesn't live here any more." Her accent was distinctly Scottish.

Preston shrugged his shoulders. "I just came back to –"

"You're one of her students aren't you?" Her eyes were quizzical.

"That's right." Preston turned to the steps.

"Aye, and you used to visit her a good many times, she told me once that she was helping you out with your maths, that true?"

Preston stared at her. "Yeah. She was my teacher, you know."

The woman rolled her eyes as she fiercely chewed some gum. "Sure that was all? Nah. You can't fool me." She made a pretence of sweeping below at her steps. "There was more to it than that, 'cause I can tell you something son –"

"Yeah, well I don't wanna hear okay?" Preston jumped down the steps. He turned in the other direction, his blood beginning to boil.

"I know a thing or two about people like you," the woman yelled, "a damn disgrace to society..... both of you need a lesson that will teach you the real moralities of the art of human life.…."

Following his feet, Preston could sense the many eyes peering at him from behind the drapes of the few suburban houses. Reaching the end of the street, he cautiously glanced behind him. The woman, leaning on her broom stick was still watching him from a long way back.

The short cloudburst was diminishing to a steady drizzle outside. Preston leaned back on the divan, trying to control his thoughts by following the show on the television. His mother had gone out to one of her social meetings, Erica was busy talking on the phone. Preston raised the volume as the programme finished.

"Here at the A.B.C. studios, is the seven o'clock news flash." Preston sipped his pepsi cola, watching the man on the screen nonchalantly. "No sign has been seen of the four youths who robbed Amberson bank yesterday evening. Police who are making –"

"Hey listen, I'm watching 'soap' on channel one." Erica flounced into the room. Immediately she switched the button.

"I was listening to that." Preston leaned forward. "I'm watching the news, Erica. Move."

She planted herself in front of the screen. "I'm watching soap."

"You want me to get mad, girl?" Preston seized her arm and pushed his finger on the last button.

"Alright, alright." Erica stood up. "What's so good about news anyway?"

Preston raised the volume again. "The youths dropped a sack of bank-rolls, but made a getaway in a green coloured beetle, after shooting dead one policeman and seriously injuring another one. The dead man, who died instantly, was named as Marvin Dwight Benjamin Kennedy, who had served with the force for –"

"May I turn back to soap now?" Erica switched back.

Preston leaned back on the divan. For a moment he felt a strange sensation; for some reason he remembered the day he had been caught in Bennison's store. He lay awake most of the night, just thinking of that.

The rain had ceased, the sun was shining. Preston lingered outside Peggy's house. He noticed with curiosity that the green drapes, suspended on the wide windows were firmly closed. The bed of roses on one side of the garden looked somewhat neglected. A few drops of rain trickled off the yellow Mercedes.

Preston found himself rehearsing a few words to say to Peggy. He glanced up. His eyes met a girl, clad in a yellow slicker; Preston recognised her as Lisa. She carried a sable-coloured bag of groceries. As she came closer he saw that her face wore a dolorous expression. Subsequently a slight smile escaped her lips. "Hello Preston."

"Hi Lisa....."

She made a tighter hold on the bag, tilting her head on one side. "I never thought I'd bump in to you again." Her voice seemed tense.

"I guess you just did." For a while they looked at one another. Automobiles rushed past them, as they stood on the side-walk. Preston let his eyes wander. "I just came by to see Peggy."

She shook her head. "I don't think she'll wanna see you right now."

"How come?" Her eyes widened.

"When your father died did you ever feel like talking to anybody?"

Preston felt a freezing douche of water trickle down his back. For a moment confusion took hold of him. Looking at Lisa he saw a light of fury in her eyes. "Hey, I can't believe this." His eyes lowered. "I mean – I listened to the news last night and heard about a Mr. Kennedy been killed – but I didn't think'd be your dad."

Their eyes met. Lisa's were awash with tears. "They're looking – the cops are looking every which way for the guys who done it."

Preston glanced away. His eyes rested on the yellow Mercedes. "I don't know what to say....."

"Don't worry." Her voice trembled. "You're not the one who's gotta say something...... it's the guys who killed my father...... they're the ones who are gonna have to say something."

Preston glanced up. She was walking back to the house. There was something very sad about her in that yellow slicker; it fitted in perfectly with the dead roses, the green drapes, the sullen house. With the damp atmosphere it made a picture of complete mourning.

A day passed. Preston was in the apartment alone. Frustration dominated his mind as he fought to complete his school assignment. For a while he found himself straying. The Michael Jackson record was playing softly in the corner of the room, he sang along with it.

"Guess I'll always be a dreamer..... dreaming my life away...... dreaming my life away." He closed his eyes, imagining he was with Mrs. Rosenberg. "I just can't wait till I go to sleep..... then I'll be with you all night long..... is it just a fantasy or is it just you, that dreaming comes my way...... ?"

The door bell rang sharply. Preston came back to reality as the ringing became persistent. He switched off the music, hurrying to the door. Ryan was standing there, in his black leather jacket, looking around a year older.

Preston stared at him, feeling a sudden pang of anger. "What're you doing here?" He stepped back, letting him step inside.

Ryan looked at him. The rims of his eyes were red, his lips were set in a droop.

"Hey, would you say something?" Preston peered closely at him. "Talk. Tell me what's the matter."

Ryan shook his head; he ran his hand through his hair. "It's – it's my brother Ashley. You heard about the bank raid?" His voice shook with tension. "He – he killed that cop, he didn't mean to. We were scared."

Preston fell back against the wall; he felt his knees weaken, he looked up to the ceiling. "Ryan." He tried to steady his voice. "You know who that cop was? You know who he was?" There was a short silence. "He was Peggy's father, that's who it was. Oh God, anything but this." Preston flashed his eyes back to Ryan. "Why..... why'd you do it?"

Flinching back, Ryan's face crumpled in rage, his eyes watered. "We never knew. We never knew. We needed the money bad..... Preston we didn't mean to kill no cop."

"Shut up. Alright. I know." Preston swiped at the air. "What're you doing back here? What're you doing hanging round here, the cops –"

"Ashley didn't mean to kill him – we're gonna cut and run – we're gonna run from this town Preston."

"You'll all be put down for good if you're caught." They stared at each other for a while. "Besides, you should be out of here by now."

Ryan was quiet. He looked away helplessly.

"Have you seen your mother?"

He raised his eyes. "She's all cut up rough on us now."

"How long do you think you're gonna run?"

"We hustled a beetle. Aaron's at the wheel." He shrugged. "We're headed to the south."

"Give yourself up Ryan. Maybe you'll get let off easy. It's Ashley that has to be scared."

"You think so?" Ryan's eyes were fierce with challenge. "He's my brother and wherever he goes I go too."

Preston went silent; he searched Ryan's face. "Where'd he get that gun?"

"Hey, you're beginning to sound like a cop yourself. Quit the questions huh?" He ran his hand over his face. "Ashley didn't mean to kill."

Preston tried to remember him. Ashley seemed so affectionate, warm hearted, he didn't look like a killer.

"If you like me Preston you won't let on to nobody that you seen me tonight." Ryan's black eyes were pleading.

Preston took a deep breath. "Listen, I like you as a brother and I don't wanna see you get hurt. You oughtn't to run, Ryan, anything's better than being chased."

Ryan brushed his hand over his eyes. "You better not let on 'cause I'm running. I ain't gonna say die, or be caught and eat crow to everybody."

"Then go. Go run, I don't care." Preston swung open the door. "You don't know what you're doing, Ryan. You'll be sorry."

Ryan suddenly turned, he threw his arms round Preston, nestling his head on his shoulder. "I want you to know something buddy. You are the first real friend that I have cared about so much."

Preston stiffened, he squeezed his eyes tight as he inhaled the smell of his leather jacket.

"There's a special bond between you and me Preston, that I don't think you'll ever come to realise."

His heart racing, Preston stared up at the ceiling.

"I love you and it's not the way I love my brothers..... it's different." Ryan raised his head, his eyes stared deeply. "I think we were made for each other, Preston, take care."

Preston threw his arms off. He glanced away. "Why'd you have to say that Ryan?"

He moved to the door. "I don't know Preston. I just did."

Preston watched as he raced down the metal steps. He followed him for a while then stopped. The green beetle screeched past him; inside it were four hunched figures. One of them turned to wave. It was Ryan.

Two days later. Tapping his bare feet to the music on the radio, Preston sipped his pepsi cola. He slowly turned the pages of the 'soul music' magazine, scanning through the latest albums. The sun was going down, it left the sky with a hazy pink complexion. The crescendo of the music stopped on the radio.

"This is the eight o'clock news flash. It has now been reported that the four youths who robbed Amberson bank on July 4th, making their get-away in a green beetle, have been caught on the north-side of San Diego highway..... complications aroused as they tried to run, and one of them was shot to death..... a spokesman for the Malibu major police department said 'one of the kids dodged the policemen and turned back unexpectedly as the hail of bullets raced through the air....we think he was probably trying to give himself up' the policeman who shot him alleged, this morning....."

Preston swallowed nervously.

"The four names given by the police are confirmed as Aaron Kassick, Kip Kassick and Ashley Kassick..... Ryan Kassick, the youngest, was thought to have died this morning in hospital..... the brothers, all under the age of twenty, were remanded at San Diego juvenile hall, all awaiting charges of robbery and murder..... further charges of car-stealing have been adjourned till later..... end of news flash."

Preston, in a trance, switched off the radio. He felt the muscles of his body suddenly quiver, as the sensation of an electric-shock travelled through him. For a moment he covered his eyes with his hand, trying to block out what he'd just heard. He banged the table with his other hand, in a mixture of anger and grief combined. Preston Wildey-King rose from the table, his head shaking, his hands covering his face, as he tried to force tears to his eyes.

A figure stood before him. "Hey Preston, what's the matter with you?" Erica's voice met his ears. "You look as though you've had an electric-shock."

Preston charged past her. He walked out the apartment, feeling a cool breeze around his shoulders. He did not feel the cool concrete beneath his bare feet, he did not see the people in the streets. Preston's thoughts were a million miles away, somewhere away with Ryan Kassick.

Preston did feel the sand as he touched the forlorn beach, he smelled the lavender air as he got closer to the sea. Remembering how he and Ryan had sat here together made his throat loosen its tightness. He stooped down scooping up some sand in his hand. "Ryan don't leave me now." His voice broke with emotion. He let the sand fall slowly through his fingers as the tears ran down his face.

Gazing out at the sea, Preston listened to the sounds of the waves smacking the shore, the distant cries of children playing, the clanking of the automobiles on the high-way. Somewhere in the lonesome sky, were the sounds of sea-gulls crying. Somewhere in the stillness of the air, the wind was quietly whispering her song of mourning.

Across the horizon, beyond the furthest clouds, lay Ryan, asleep peacefully..... in a world of golden silence. Preston lay down on the sand and closed his eyes as the tears forced themselves out. For a while he shivered as the foamy water lapped over his feet. The stars showed themselves in the ebony of the darkness. Preston listened to the sobs of the dying sea, he listened to the sobs from his own throat, all night long.

A painful light attacked his eyes. Preston felt the dampness of water around him, the morning sun shone down on him. A slim figure was headed toward him; she shouted out his name, then began to run. Erica's face was deeply flushed with vitality. "Preston..... we've been out nearly all night looking for you." Preston rose stiffly, as she put a warm arm round his shoulders. "You're just absolutely soaked." For a while they walked entwined through the sand. Erica lowered her face to his. "You like the beach so much that you decide to sleep here huh..... I'm sorry about Ryan..... it came as such a shock, me and mom heard about him on the news..... I'm sorry."

Preston lay in the warmth of his bed, most of the following days. He lay there thinking about Ryan. He day-dreamed about Ryan's funeral. Flowers and wreaths lining his casket, just like his father's had been. Mrs. Kassick in a dark veil, crying helplessly; Aaron, Kip and Ashley, wearing best suits, standing grief-stricken. Preston thought; life is a confusement. Why do all the people I know have to always go away?

Preston combed his hair in the mirror, the morning sun dazzled through the open window. A while later he was picking the phone up, with a feeling of hope as he dialled Peggy's number. A silence followed as someone picked up the receiver.

"Hello, may I talk to Peggy please." Preston waited, he listened. There was an obstructive sound of a long shirring. He knew the phone was dead. Blindly, he ambled into the kitchen, pulling open the refrigerator. He ripped off the ring and drank back a pepsi cola.

Saturday evening. The apartment was filled with summer silence. Preston gazed through the kitchen window at the slowly diminishing sun. He threw his untouched cheese-cake into the plastic trash-can. Erica came into the room, clad in skin-tight jeans, turquoise halter-neck top. Her brunette hair cascaded down her shoulders in thick natural waves.

"Hi Prezz, what's new?" she smiled. "I'm going out in a moment."

Preston sat down at the table and took a gulp of his pepsi cola. "Where to?"

He watched as she opened the refrigerator. Pulling out a celery stick, she sucked on it hungrily. "I'm going to the baseball match." The sound of vigorous munching. "You care to come?..... it's the Root-higs versus the Bush-whackers."

Preston shrugged. She came over to sit on the table, a scent rising in the air.

"Who you going with?"

"The same bunch of girls." She munched again. "You wanna come?"

"I don't think so."

Erica jumped off the table. "You know, you're as dead as the do-do." She threw half the celery in the trash can. "But I've got other fish to fry. When mom gets back from work, tell her where I've gone, okay?"

The door slammed as she went out. Preston listened to her footsteps, he listened to a car draw up, then it roared off in the distance.

A while later, with three pepsi colas at his side, he was watching the last series of 'The Dukes of Hazzards'. The telephone rang cutting into his thoughts. He answered it. "Yeah, hello?"

"This is Mrs. Wildey-King I hope?" A woman's nasal, no-nonsense voice came over the wire.

"You have the right house, alright, but I'm her son." He interrupted. "No I'm sorry but she's not home from work yet."

"Child, it's important that I talk to her."

Preston scratched his head. "Can you leave a message, then please?"

There was a pause. "I don't think so. Listen, I'll phone tomorrow again."

"Was it important? I can write it down on paper."

"Don't bother, just say Mrs. Kasanki phoned, she'll know who I mean."

"Alright." Preston put the receiver back in its cradle. He stood there for a while gazing at it. He picked it up again and dialled Peggy's number. He felt a singing sensation at the pit of his stomach.

"Hello?"

"Who is this?" A familiar voice replied. Preston recognised it as Lisa's.

"It's me.... Preston." There was a silence.

"This is Lisa...... thanks for phoning...I haven't been able to talk to anybody for days."

Preston tapped the phone timidly. "You're having a hard time, I guess."

"Peggy swooned at the funeral..... she was very close to him..... she's having a harder time than me."

Preston had a sudden vision of her. He had lost two people close to him, in a lifetime, so she had lost one. Her father.

"You still there?..... the Kassicks are all across the front of the newspapers. I read all about..... I'm kinda sorry about Ryan though...I never knew the guy until they mentioned where he went to school."

A melancholy feeling roused inside Preston. "I didn't swoon at my father's funeral.... I just cried, you know."

" ....I didn't even do that....it was strange, but I just couldn't, know what I mean?..... me. I just thought about the good times we had together..... I didn't even listen to what the priest said.... 'cause I just hate funerals."

There was a pause. "I guess you feel as though the biggest part of you has been taken away from you..... right?"

"..... I don't know Preston. Maybe. Did you feel that way once?"

Preston nodded his head absently. "Yeah, and it's funny like, 'cause I still do."

"Funny that..... you never seem to know how much you love somebody until they actually die..... you get to appreciate them more."

"I guess that's true." Preston felt suddenly cold.

"I know.... it's the same way I feel about my dad now."

".... same way I feel about Ryan too."

There was a pause. "..... I hope that when I die someday, somebody'll feel that way about me too.... yes mom, coming..... I have to go now, Preston. Thanks for caring and listening."

"Don't thank me about this Lisa, it's something that everybody does once in a lifetime." He took the receiver from his ear, placing it back in its cradle. "Or maybe twice." He shrugged his shoulders. For a while he forgot about Peggy.

During the days to come, Preston began to grow somewhat depressed over himself. The nightmares that visited him each time he slept drove him to a point of desperation, so that he tried to stay awake all night.

During one hot night, Preston fell asleep. He was in a pool of pepsi cola. The refreshing flavour washed down his throat and as he tried to swim, he splashed around the warm liquid. From an open sunlit cave, somebody called his name. Turning around, Preston felt the strength drain from him. Three gigantic pepsi cola cans were headed his way, drifting rapidly to him. They surrounded him, they squashed him, he gasped for air. Abruptly they transformed. Mrs. Rosenberg put her hands tightly round his throat, Ryan dragged him under, he laughed. As Preston struggled, he glanced up. Peggy was smiling down at him, before he felt the liquid run over him..... He awoke with a sudden jerk, the sun shining powerfully on his face. He was sweating profusely. The dime-store clock read half of ten. Weakly he rose from his bed, the weight of his body dragging him back slightly. He staggered through empty pepsi cola cans to the door. His mother's voice reached his ears as she talked on the phone. "Yes Mrs. Kasanki. No. Tupperware party? I'll let you know....."

Turning on the faucet in the bathroom, Preston momentarily saw brown pepsi cola splash into the basin;

he washed his face, remembering the dream. He examined his face in the onyx mirror, pulled on a clean tee shirt, then headed to the kitchen.

Mrs. Wildey-King was turning on a faucet to fill a saucepan. She looked at him as he opened the refrigerator for a pepsi cola.

"Preston you know, you're forever drinking that stuff." She put the pan on the cooker, staring at him anxiously. "I'm taking you to a doctor, don't ask me why, but I am."

Preston felt a freezing sensation. "Just because I drink this stuff?"

"I just don't like the way you look." Her voice seemed concerned. She ran her hand through her corrugated hair. "You really do look depressed...... I know it's natural for boys your age to feel that way sometimes.... but you look sick."

"Listen mom, I'm perfectly okay." Preston took a gulp of pepsi cola.

"I don't know how you can say that, you don't even eat." She nervously struck a match to a cigarette, taking a deep draw. "In fact all you do is drink."

"Mom that's my business."

"To hell with what's your business." Her eyes blazed. "You look like one of those goddam moonies."

Preston squeezed the can in his hand. "So what, huh?"

"Don't say that. You're going to a doctor come Monday and that's flat."

"You gonna make me?"

She stared at him. "There's no way you're gonna change my mind. I'll take you there even if I have to drag you."

Monday morning game. Preston stood in front of the mirror, combing his hair. His mother flounced into the room. "Preston would you hurry up. The time is just after nine, we have to be there at fifteen minutes past."

They entered the large Malibu state hospital. Preston began to feel uncomfortable as he smelled the aroma of disinfectant; it reminded him of the agonising days he'd spent in prison. The orderlies in their white creepers ambled past him, a nurse pushed an old man in a wheel chair, his face lost to the world.

Preston followed his mother into one of the glass partitioned waiting rooms, they sat on white foam-padded chairs. There was a large crowd of people sitting opposite them; one of them was a girl about fifteen, and Preston let his eyes rest on her. She had fair short-cropped hair, which surrounded her elfin like face. A moment passed; her hazel eyes suddenly caught Preston's. He glanced away.

The door marked Dr. Kendon's surgery opened. A stout man in a car-jacket ambled out, followed by a man in white. Dr. Kendon placed his hands in his pockets, looked straight at Preston, then to his mother.

"Mrs. Wildey-King?"

"Yes.... that's me."

"Won't you come in?"

A moment later they were sitting in easy chairs opposite him. The doctor twirled his chair around, behind the mahogany desk, to face them. Sunlight streamed in through the large window, making a sheet of dust visible in the air.

"Now Preston," the man sat up straight, "your mother here, tells me that you're depressed. Is that true?"

Preston shrugged. "I know if I'm depressed or not, and I'm not."

His mother eyed him sternly. "Then what's the matter with you?"

"Maybe you ought to tell me about yourself Preston." The doctor leaned forward. He looked about fifty, his head was massive, his hands hirsute, a fringe of white peroxided hair clung to his forehead.

Preston glanced away. "There's nothing to tell."

"Oh sure there is," put in Mrs. Wildey-King, "tell him about your friend Ryan, how you broke into a store, how you spent time down the joint."

There was a painful silence. Preston felt his armpits go wet, his mouth dry.

"Who's Ryan?" the doctor inquired.

Preston swallowed hard. "He was a friend."

"What sort of a friend? Where is he now?"

"Why are you asking me all these questions?"

"I'm here to help you."

"Like hell. I don't need any help." Preston moved restlessly in the chair. He caught his mother's eye. "You're the one who brought me here mom, and I told you I'm not depressed."

"Then what are you feeling right now?" Dr. Kendon's voice was doubtful.

"That I may be wasting my time here." Preston stood up suddenly. "Listen may I go now?"

The doctor's face changed. "Yes Preston, if you really don't need my help."

Mrs. Wildey-King rose. "Preston? I brought you here for a –"

"Then forget it mom." He turned to the door.

Dr. Kendon came over to him. He gazed at him hopefully. "Here you are Preston, take this card, this is the telephone number to my surgery if you should need me –"

"I'll take that." Mrs. Wildey-King outstretched her palm to receive the white card. "Thank you, I'll make sure Preston comes next week Dr. Kendon."

Pulling the door open, Preston charged out. He did not see the people sitting alongside the wall. His thoughts were faraway as he walked rapidly down the shiny corridors, up the elevator and out the hospital at last.

A day later, after hours of thinking, he telephoned Peggy.

"Hello, may I talk to Peggy please?"

There was a pause. "This is she."

Preston's heart palpitated. "Peggy, when can I see you again, huh?"

"Preston, I thought I told you we were through."

"I'm not through with you.... you know that?"

"That's your business." Her voice was strained. "You know what I'm gonna do now.... ? I'm gonna hang up on you."

"Wait." Preston tried to control his anxiety. "Can't we just meet in the park sometime..... tomorrow?"

"What good is it, huh?"

"I don't know.... but please, just say yes..... I'll meet you at five..... will you be there?"

"Why.... yes, okay, I'll try, but remember.... don't phone me again." The phone went dead. Preston smiled.

The sun was a blanket of warmness as Preston sat on the park bench the next evening. He listened to the shouts of children as they played frisbee on the grass. He watched the automobiles whizz past the gates. Preston glanced at his watch; a shadow passed his face, he let his arms drop to his sides. A long while later he sat up, he saw a blonde haired girl walking toward him; it was not Peggy. Leaning back on the bench, Preston closed his eyes, praying in his heart that she would come. The shouts of children diminished, the automobiles stopped coming.

Preston opened his eyes; the sky had become a fiery red, the sun was hiding behind a distant mountain. With his finger-nail he scratched carefully Peggy's name on the wooden bench. Beside it he placed a love-heart, then he scratched his own name. He walked home.

He was lying on his bed, a hot iron rod resting on his back. He gazed up at the ceiling. Preston thought about Peggy, he imagined she was beside him. Caressing himself, he felt a cold sweat break out, a tightening between his legs. He un-buckled the belt to his levis. An urgent feeling of desire came over him. He toyed with his genitals until he felt relief flooding through him. Thunder split through his ear-drums, his bedroom door flew open. Preston jerked up. His mother walked in.

"Preston, what are you doing?.... what're you doing in bed at this time of day.... huh?"

Preston buckled his belt up as he jumped off the bed. He stared at his mother hotly.

"I told you, today is Wednesday and you're going to keep that appointment with the doctor." She thrust forward the white card.

"What appointment?" Preston snatched the card from her hand. "I'm not going to no crap doctor."

"Yes you damn well are, he's expecting you right now."

Preston shook his head. "You think you can tell me what's wrong with me? You think you can bust in here when you like and –"

"I can tell you that you're going." She flounced over to him. "Get up, get out and go to that doctor."

"Get off me, you're not gonna make me see no rotten quack." Preston flinched backwards. "You've just about had it." He ripped at the card in his hand, each tear increasing his anger, until he let the pieces fly in the air.

He felt a sharp blow to his face, a stinging, searing pain on his left jaw, and the tears rushed to his eyes. His mother was standing before him, her eyes held a strange powerful look, her hand was still raised. "Now get out to that damn doctor."

"Or what? You gonna hit me again?" Preston seized his tee shirt on the bed. He charged past her, knocking her back slightly. "Where you going?" she screamed.

"Not to the doctor, just somewhere to get away from you."

"I'm gonna make another appointment for you next Wednesday, so you're not gonna walk out on me like that.... Preston?..... Preston?"

Preston walked to the beach, the breeze in the air calmed his anger.

On Saturday he was on the beach again, his mind beyond the marine, crystal sea. He felt a hand on his shoulder, and turned around. Smiling at him assuredly was Peggy. Preston felt a provocative sensation around in him as he looked at her. Her large blue eyes expressed sadness, her hair blew lightly with the fresh afternoon breeze.

"Hello Preston."

"Hello Peggy."

She crossed her arms protectively across her chest. For a moment she gazed at him. "You're not gonna ask why I failed to show up at the park Tuesday?"

Preston lowered his eyes. "You didn't want to see me?"

"I did wanna see you," she replied sardonically. An aroma of honey suckle rose in the air. "I had no time, I guess.... I was busy?"

Preston raised his eyes. "You were busy?"

"I was packing my suitcase.... Preston, we've decided to leave Malibu." She made nervous darts with her eyes, until they rested on her clam-diggers.

"We're gonna live in San-Francisco – it'll be nice there..... it hurts for us to stay here."

As he caught his breath, Preston felt a sharp pang of surprise, and indignation as though she had slapped him in the face. "What – what are you saying?"

Peggy glanced up. "I'm saying that I'm leaving – so don't give me a hard time Preston." A light irritation passed her eyes. "Don't tell me that I'm hurting your feelings. Because I'm not talking about my father's death."

Preston tried to hold on to the muscles of his face. "Peggy..... what about us? How can you say you're not talking about me?"

She glanced away, her hand to her face. "What about us?..... we like each other, love each other. We can love other people too – can't we?"

"Wait a moment – I don't understand you."

She flashed him a look of severity. "You never did. You never even tried to understand me. So that's not new to me."

The happy laughter of children echoed in a nearby cove. The smack of the waves on the shoreline sounded like a sheet of glass breaking. Preston looked at the profile of Peggy. His eyes began to sting.

"We can write each other," she murmured resolutely. "We can keep contact..... become pen-pals."

"I'm not much good at writing."

Their eyes suddenly met. "Have you still got the photographs I gave you?"

Preston felt suddenly afraid of her unemotional voice. He glanced away resting his eyes on the sea, feeling her eyes on him.

"Yours is on my dresser," she continued, "beside the mirror. You're there smiling at me, each time I brush my hair."

Preston counted the blobs of white foam floating aimlessly on the green water.

"Why you mad at me Preston?" Their shoulders touched. "I didn't mean for this to happen....."

"I'm not mad."

"Then why.... ?" She moved away, her hand running through her hair, her voice deafened by the waves. "Why won't you look at me and say goodbye?.... I didn't come here to fight. We're just two great friends, okay? Let me leave, with that kind of feeling inside me."

Preston turned around. His eyes were brimming with tears, and he clenched his jaws ineffectually, to calm his trembling lips. "Okay.... but Peggy I happen to love you. Don't you care about what happens to me, what I feel?"

Peggy moved abruptly closer; tears trickled down her face as she took Preston's hand. He slid his arm around her waist, pressing his body against hers, squeezing her tight, as though he'd never let her go.

She struggled, her arms pushing him away. "I feel the same way you feel."

Preston stepped closer, he put his hand to her face. She looked up, moving closer until their lips touched. She responded for a moment, then she suddenly broke off. "Goodbye Preston." The wind blew through her hair as she backed away.

Preston let his hand drop to his side. "Wait Peggy."

She turned away abruptly. The sea-gulls cried out pitifully in the sky, as she ran swiftly up the beach, through the sand, getting further away all the time. Preston watched, until he could only see a speck of gold, bobbing among the distant crowds. He turned away to the sea, thinking he must be dreaming. It's all a dream.... I'm feeling cold..... I'll soon be awake. Laughter of children nearby broke the spell. As the tears touched his hands, Preston stared up at the sky for a long while, until the sun blinded his eyes.

Racing out the school gates, dodging crowds in the city, Preston stopped breathlessly outside Malibu state hospital. He pushed open the glass swing doors, a feeling of determination coming over him as he walked over to the counter.

A young nurse looked up from a log book with an expression of concern about her tiny face. "May I help you?"

"I'd like to cancel my appointment with Dr. Kendon," Preston said hurriedly. The nurse closed the book. "What time is he expecting you please?"

Preston looked past her. "Around half four."

She looked at him warily. "And may I have your name?"

Preston watched as she wrote his name down on a yellow slip. She glanced up. "Would you like me to put you down for another appointment – if so what time and day would that be?"

Preston shrugged. A sudden vision of his apartment loomed in his mind. "I don't think I'll be needing any more appointments." He turned abruptly, heading for the glass doors.

Outside the hospital, Preston looked up at the soot-covered tenements, he looked down at the grey side-walks, scanned the colourful automobiles that whizzed past him. Bags of un-collected garbage lined the streets, bags that were beige, yellow, green or blue. Most of the bags were torn open by rats, spilling out half the waste of Malibu city, from messy ice-cream tubs, to empty pepsi cola cans. Preston ran, kicked, then sent a can squealing into the street.

He ambled over to a yellow truck, parked carelessly on the side-walk. On the back of it was a poster from a coca cola commercial. Two people, a man and woman, were both wearing red tee shirts, bearing the coca cola trade mark. Both of them were drinking from cans. Beneath them, Preston read the bold white words. "ENJOY YOUR COCA COLA: 'CAUSE COKE ADDS LIFE AND EVERYBODY NEEDS A LITTLE LIFE".

"A little life," Preston repeated sarcastically. "A little life. Who needs life?" He shrugged his shoulders, walking on. The hot afternoon sun was a fireball in the sky, a gentle breeze cooled the sultry air. Across the street a boy and a girl were walking together, sharing a can of pepsi cola between them. Preston eyed the girl cautiously, pain stabbed in his head as he thought of Peggy. He let his eyes fall ahead of him; a burly man was carrying a crate of pepsi colas into a nearby drug-store. Preston ran past him, he ran all the way until he reached the steps of the apartment. He stopped by the door. For a while he just stood there. The gentle cry of a baby strayed through the window of another apartment. Preston tore the key from around his neck, and opened the door, slamming it shut behind him.

The apartment was filled with the lonesome atmosphere of a sleeping cemetery. The buzzing sound coming from the refrigerator turned to a deep sigh as Preston opened it to yank out a pepsi cola. He turned to the window, taking large gulps of the liquid as he stared out to space.

A moment later, his hands were rummaging through the cupboard; they did not seem to belong to him. His eyes swept over the bottles of food, medicine and powdered milk. Preston was wondering why his mother kept so many pills. He reached over for the bottle of barbiturates. Closing the cupboard, Preston unscrewed the lid and poured the tablets into his palm, throwing the bottle in the trash-can.

The telephone began to peal. Preston stopped still in the corridor, his heart raced; anxiously he thought about Peggy; she was a million miles away. He let the phone ring. In his room, Preston stared at his blank face in the mirror, he wiped his eyes. Strolling over to the window, he closed the drapes so that the sun disappeared, leaving the room in a hazy darkness. Preston sat down on his bed, and stared hard at the pills in his hand. Like a tape-recorder voices began to talk in his mind; his eyes pulled away to look at the graffiti of 'PEGGY' on the bedroom door. For a while he murmured her name, for a while he stared at the pills in his palm. Preston drew a deep breath, he crammed the pills into his mouth, feeling the bitter taste; his body jerked in a series of wracking sobs. He munched hard, swallowing with gulps the pepsi cola that washed down his throat, like a burning fire.

Preston lay back in bewilderment. For a moment he wondered where the pills had gone. Frantically he listened to the thumps of his heart, and he placed his hands over his stomach.

His eyes darted nervously, he was looking through a telescope, the walls were closing in, pop-stars gazed down at him, a body lying on a bed. From far away, the distant sound of a telephone grew louder on each ring. Preston felt his body jolt, heavy thoughts raced through his mind, urgent thoughts of Peggy. The telephone rang, it rang, it cried out. Lifting his numb head, Preston sat up, his legs like lead, he was walking on air. The floor was a synthetic sponge, it dragged him down. Preston was blinded for a moment by hot tears that ran down his face. For some reason he had to get to that phone.

Standing unsteadily in the corridor, Preston swayed over to the ringing phone; he picked up the receiver, the perspiration heavy on his hands.

"Hello.... ?"

"Preston, is that you?" Peggy's voice attacked his ears. His knees began to weaken, his voice slurred. "Peggy?"

"Listen, I have to tell you something..... Preston, we're not leaving Malibu.... are you listening?..... I love you. I can't go to San Francisco."

A knife so sharp, it sliced into Preston's heart. The pain deafened his ear-drums. He sank to the floor, the phone crashing down beside him. Only a murmuring of a girl's voice screamed out in the distance. "Preston? Preston can you hear me?" Preston was swinging on the magic swing of freedom, it got faster, faster, faster, faster, spinning into an unknown world. He was falling, floating in an empty black tunnel..... like a rocket trapped in space, a can of pepsi cola came twisting and turning toward him.... it crashed....Preston slept.

Outside, below the steps, at this moment, three young boys were playing kick-the-can with an empty pepsi cola can. It had fallen from the over-piled trash-can, parked in a nearby corner. The smallest of the dark-haired boys made a big kick, the can rolled away. "I love pepsi cola," he yelled. Jumping up, he raced after the can. The two other boys strolled away; the small boy stared down at the can. Some remaining liquid slowly trickled out, emerging onto the street. He stooped down, dabbed his finger into it, then ran aimlessly down the street, licking it.

The pepsi cola stopped running as it came to the edge of the street. It lay there invisible to all passers-by, where it dried up silently under the radiation of the burning sun.

THE END

Publisher's Note:

June-Alison Gibbons desired that this edition should be true to the book that she created as a 16-year-old girl, with its sometimes idiosyncratic and inconsistent spelling, hyphenation, and punctuation. Working with David Tibet and Ania Goszczyńska, June-Alison has corrected obvious typos made by the original publishers, who re-typed June-Alison's own typescript when laying it out. The text is now faithful to how she originally wrote it.

Afterword: Notes on the Pepsi Cola Addict
Chris Mikul

Marjorie Wallace's 1986 book *The Silent Twins*, and a BBC TV documentary of the same name, introduced the world to the extraordinary story of June-Alison and Jennifer Gibbons. Born in 1963, the identical twins were the daughters of Aubrey and Gloria Gibbons, who migrated to the UK from Barbados and eventually settled in Haverfordwest, Wales.

Inseparable from birth, as children June-Alison and Jennifer had ceased to speak to others – so that even their parents and older brother and sister were lucky to receive a single grunted word (their little sister Rosie was the only exception, although they stopped speaking to her, too, when she was eleven). When in the presence of others, the twins did everything in unison and extremely slowly, observing each other constantly, as if neither one ever wanted to make the first move. When alone, they spoke to each other incredibly quickly – the sound was likened to the twittering of birds – and most assumed that they had invented their own language. Later, when tape recordings of their speech were slowed down, it was found that they were speaking English, but with very unusual pronunciations. They had also been born with a speech impediment which, June-Alison later explained, was the reason they had stopped speaking to others in the first place.

The twins' silence and slowness made them very unpopular at school, and they were often set upon by other children. When this happened, they would cling together stoically, arms around each other's shoulders. Their situation eventually came to the attention of the education authorities, and in 1976 they were placed in a special school called the Eastgate Centre. After two years, the staff had made little progress with them – they would write things down but still resolutely refused to speak to anyone – and it was decided to separate them. Most of those who had observed them noted that June-Alison was the more intelligent and creative of the two, but it was Jennifer who played the dominant role in keeping them bound together. Perhaps surprisingly, it was the twins who first suggested they should be separated – it seems they were as frustrated by their situation as everyone else. But the reality of separation proved devastating, and they were reunited.

The twins left Eastgate at the end of 1979 and retreated into the bedroom they shared with Rosie. They rarely left it, and communicated with their parents via notes. Here they spent much of their time playing with dolls, which they gave names and personalities, acting out elaborate, often violent storylines and recording some of them on tape. The stories were invariably set in America, a country which fascinated the twins. They decided they were going to become writers, took a correspondence course in creative writing, read the classics voraciously, and began writing stories, poems and plays at a rapid rate. In January 1980, June-Alison started her first novel, *The Pepsi-Cola Addict*, and completed it just over a month later. The twins pooled their dole money and in 1981 paid a vanity press, New Horizon, £499.50 to print 185 copies of the book (without bothering to tell their parents about it). Inspired by June-Alison's effort, Jennifer wrote a strange little novella, *The Pugilist*, about a doctor who, fearing that his young son will die from a heart condition, transplants into him the heart of the family's pet dog. She followed this up with *Discomania*, a tale of juvenile delinquency set in the near future.

The twins sent their manuscripts to various publishers, but were rejected by all of them. They were depressed by this, and growing tired of their insular life. They were fighting a lot, and June-Alison once tried to drown Jennifer in a river. At the same time they were becoming interested in boys, and hooked up with Jerry, Wayne and Carl Kennedy, the sons of an American naval officer stationed in Wales, who introduced them to alcohol, drugs and sex. The girls were devastated when the boys returned to America, and began to go off the rails, embarking on a mini crime spree of shoplifting, breaking and entering, vandalism and arson (including setting fire to a tractor store which caused £100,000 worth of damage). It was such a small town, and the twins had such a reputation for weirdness, that they were soon caught. They had been so brazen – ringing the police from payphones, for example – that it seems part of them wanted it to happen.

The twins spent over a year in remand, during which time their relationship deteriorated further, yet they were unable to break away from each other, and still found it almost impossible to communicate with anyone else. In May 1983, on the advice of their defence team, they pleaded guilty to the property damage charges. While this saved them from prison, they were instead sent to Broadmoor psychiatric hospital for an indefinite period. They had fantasised about how good life would be in there, so the reality of Broadmoor, the home to psychopaths like Ronnie Kray and Peter Sutcliffe, was a shock.

The twins were placed in separate wards, but they conspired to be together as much as possible, and remained locked in the same destructive love/hate relationship. Their thoughts, recorded in copious diary entries, continued to revolve around each other, although they made some fumbling attempts to build relationships with others. After several years they were put on heavy doses of tranquillisers, which did unlock their tongues to some extent, but also took away most of their desire to write – their only real form of communication. They believed that once they started speaking they would be released, but the years went by, and it wasn't until just before their thirtieth birthday that they were told they would be moving to a minimum-security facility in Wales. By now, they had decided that the only solution to their predicament was for one of them to die, and they argued about who it should be. It seems a decision was made. When Marjorie Wallace visited them around this time, Jennifer, who looked thin and unwell, told her, "I'm going to die".

On 9 March 1993 the twins boarded a mini-bus which drove them through the gates of Broadmoor, where they had spent the last eleven years. During the journey, Jennifer fell asleep with her head resting on June-Alison's shoulder. When they arrived at the facility in Wales, she did not regain consciousness, and was taken to a hospital where she died half an hour later. The post-mortem found that her death was caused by 'acute myocarditis', a severe inflammation of the heart muscle.

June-Alison's *The Pepsi-Cola Addict* was the only work created by the twins during their period of frenzied literary activity which was published, and fewer than ten copies of that original edition are known to exist today. (A contract was signed with New Horizon to publish Jennifer's last book, *The Taxi-Driver's Son*, but when the publishers wrote to her in 1982 and received no reply – the twins were by then in remand – they destroyed the manuscript.)

The Pepsi-Cola Addict would have been quite an achievement for any sixteen-year-old, but when you consider June-Alison's unique circumstances, it's little short of extraordinary. She worked hard to make the American setting convincing, peppering it with cultural references picked up from books and television, and while there are inevitably some slips, she did manage to convey a picture of Malibu during a long hot summer surprisingly well. It's a juvenile work, of course, full of odd turns of phrase and words that aren't always used correctly (yet it is never unintentionally funny – June-Alison's seriousness of purpose is too evident throughout). And somehow this awkwardness of style complements the subject matter and reinforces the inner turmoil of her intensely imagined hero, Preston Wildey-King.

From *Biblio Curiosa* #1, 2011

Acknowledgements by the publishers of the Cashen's Gap edition

We would like to thank June-Alison Gibbons for her enormous kindness, and great trust – she has been a delight to work with on every step of this project. We are also immensely grateful to: Daniel Wilson; Chris Mikul, who made us a copy of his own first edition before we finally obtained one for ourselves; Tristan Proctor of The Antique Map and Bookshop in Puddletown, Dorset, who found that first edition for us; Ossian Brown, Geoff Cox; Mark Pilkington and Jamie Sutcliffe of Strange Attractor Press; Bea Turner for transcribing the text and Maïa Gaffney-Hyde for laying the book out. We would also like to thank, with love, Gloria Gibbons, June-Alison and Jennifer's remarkable and inspirational mother.

This project has been an obsession of love for us for many years. Firstly, we had to find a copy of the first edition of *The Pepsi-Cola Addict*. We swiftly realised that to do that, we needed to find June-Alison Gibbons. Once we were in touch with her, thanks to Daniel Wilson, we—very patiently—waited for June-Alison to give us her Queenly permission.

It means more to us than we can spell that we have played a small part in bringing this unearthly book, and the unearthly creative brilliance of June-Alison and Jennifer, back into this unearthly world once again. We love you always, June-Alison and Jennifer!

Ania Goszczyńska and David Tibet, 7 February 2023

STRANGE ATTRACTOR PRESS 2023